Sophie needed no further prompting

She raised her arms, winding them around her husband's neck and let her fingers sink into his dark hair as he drew her fully into his embrace. It was as though her mind and body, starved of comfort and numbed by the anxieties of the past few hours, had found sanctuary and were now happy to lose themselves in their uncharacteristically erotic response to that intimately exploring mouth.

Only after the priest coughed discreetly for the second time did Patrick Carlisle draw back from the slim clinging figure of his wife. Puzzled amusement lurked in the exotic green depths of his eyes as he gazed down at her.

"Who'd have guessed," he said, chuckling softly, "that a hot-blooded siren lay buried beneath that frumpy exterior...."

KATE PROCTOR is a British writer who has lived abroad most of her adult life. Now divorced, she lives in London with her two grown-up daughters and her cat, Wellington. She is a qualified French teacher, but at present devotes all her time to writing.

Books by Kate Proctor

HARLEQUIN PRESENTS
1195—SWEET CAPTIVITY
1253—WILD ENCHANTMENT
1292—RECKLESS HEART

KATE PROCTOR

lawfully wedded stranger

Harlequin Books

TORONTO • NEW YORK • LONDON
AMSTERDAM • PARIS • SYDNEY • HAMBURG
STOCKHOLM • ATHENS • TOKYO • MILAN

Harlequin Presents first edition August 1991
ISBN 0-373-11389-7

Original hardcover edition published in 1990
by Mills & Boon Limited

LAWFULLY WEDDED STRANGER

CHAPTER ONE

'PATRICK JUAN-CARLOS...'

Sophie Drysdale gave a slight start as the soft words of the priest penetrated her mind. She was almost asleep on her feet again, she remonstrated anxiously with herself...she really ought to make more effort to concentrate.

Patrick Juan-Carlos. She turned the name over in her mind. That second name, she supposed, went some way to explaining why an Irishman—an apparent Irishman, she corrected herself—was actually a Spaniard...or travelled on a Spanish passport anyway. Striving to find something less taxing and confusing with which to occupy her mind, Sophie surreptitiously pushed the heavy dark glasses higher up the bridge of her nose, wincing as her hand made clumsy contact with the swollen contours of her face. At least the antibiotics would soon take care of that, she comforted herself, her eyes straying now to seek out the friendly figure of the Russian journalist who had so miraculously provided her with them. Her eyes dropped almost immediately, their attempt to make distinction between any of the shadowy figures in the room rendered virtually impossible by the dark lenses of the glasses.

She winced again as the tall, statuesquely built man beside her gave her a sharp nudge. It was the second time during the proceedings that Patrick Carlisle's elbow had made vigorous contact with her ribs, she

5

thought petulantly—a third such blow and she would more than likely keel over.

'He's asking whether you do or don't.' Though there was discernible humour in the man's tone, it was a humour liberally sprinkled with impatience. Yet, despite his having whispered the words, noted her drifting thoughts, there could be no mistaking that familiar, intriguing blend of Irish and English in his accent that made Patrick Carlisle's voice so instantly identifiable.

After twice having to clear her throat, Sophie eventually managed to recite her hastily memorised responses, only to be startled into more positive wakefulness by the muted though decidedly derisive cheer suddenly breaking out around them.

The anger in the warning look he directed towards his colleagues darkened the remarkable green of Patrick Carlisle's eyes several shades as he reached for Sophie with a muttered oath.

'Can't those jokers see the embassy staff are edgy enough about this without having their suspicions added to like this? We'd best see if we can put His Majesty's Ambassador's mind at rest.'

As Sophie's mind silently battled with sorting out precisely what it was that was making it so vital that the Spanish Ambassador's mind be put at rest, the arm Patrick Carlisle suddenly slipped round her waist scattered those thoughts, returning her to the state which had been her most familiar that day—one of knowing that soon she would have to wake, because this weird dream, with all its disturbingly sinister undertones, could hardly go on forever.

The arm around her held her firmly, which was just as well because in the instant a pair of determined lips covered hers Sophie felt her knees buckle from out-right shock.

'Come on, you'll have to do better than that!' he exclaimed impatiently against her tightly clamped mouth. 'Put a bit of enthusiasm into kissing the groom.'

The groom! This morning she had woken as usual to the peaceful sounds of rural Gamborran life in the small clinic that had been her workplace and home for the past eight months. Even the horrors of the viral conjunctivitis she had contracted almost a month before, and which had so swiftly and painfully re-versed her role from that of nurse to one of patient, had not been able to detract too drastically from her pleasure in her now familiar African surroundings. But shortly after she had woken today, her mind still battling sluggishly against the sedatives Sister Magda had been administering for several days, her peaceful world was disintegrating around her... Sister Beatrice's tears as she had told her of the terrible hap-penings in the country; of the drunken act of arson that had recently destroyed part of the clinic; of the sisters' decision that she must leave immediately be-cause today's flight from the capital would be the last for the foreseeable future. And it was here, at the Spanish Embassy in the tiny capital where she had been passed into the hands of strangers—top-notch news reporters, she had learned—that her mind had withdrawn in self-protection from the heated debate over, of all things, the fact that her passport had been destroyed together with the rest of her possessions in the clinic fire. She should have paid a lot more at-tention, she thought nervously ...it was all because of her passport that the man beside her was her groom!

She had just married a complete stranger! The fact that Patrick Carlisle's job as a roving foreign correspondent made his fascinating hybrid accent and disproportionate good looks familiar to her and to innumerable other members of the television viewing public was neither here nor there. No matter how familiar his face—the man was a complete and utter stranger to her. Yet it was no wonder she was convinced this was a dream, observed her beleaguered mind as that familiar, quite devastatingly attractive face loomed into focus ... and what the hell? If this really was a dream, she might just as well enjoy the good parts of it!

It was her gasp of surprise, as she felt his lips try to prise open hers, that made any further effort on his part unnecessary. Then it was not so much surprise as a tingling shock of pleasure she was experiencing as his mouth began a thorough and quite disconcertingly intimate exploration of hers.

With no further prompting on his part, Sophie raised her arms, winding them around her husband's neck and letting her fingers sink into the heavy darkness of his hair as he drew her fully into his arms. It was as though her mind and body, starved of comfort and numbed by the anxieties of the past few hours, had found sanctuary and were now happy to lose themselves in their uncharacteristically erotic response to the careless sensuality of that intimately exploring mouth.

It was only after the second of the discreet coughs given by the priest that Patrick Carlisle drew back from the slim, clinging figure of his wife—puzzled amusement lurking in the exotic green depths of his dark-lashed eyes as he gazed down at her.

'Who'd have guessed a hot-blooded siren lay buried beneath that frumpy exterior?' he chuckled softly, releasing her as the Ambassador approached their side.

There was a constrained smile on the Spaniard's face as he stretched out his hand to the still chuckling groom and began speaking in soft-toned, rapid Spanish.

Her inability to understand a word of what was being said could hardly have been further from Sophie's mind as her feelings of disorientation and the debilitating exhaustion which had earlier threatened to overcome her were swept aside in a welter of outraged indignation. The man had actually referred to her as frumpy!

Completely thrown by that casually damning word, she glanced down at the faded blue cotton dress Sister Beatrice had handed her only that morning... All right, so she was dressed in a nun's cast-offs, she accepted wryly, then gave a half-hearted smile. It was men's often too positive reaction to her looks that sometimes made her decidedly wary towards them, she reminded herself—so why get in a tizz just because Patrick Carlisle hadn't responded like most? Even as the thought trickled through her mind another followed close on its heels. Her hand rose to her cheek, her fingers exploring its tender, swollen contours. Her face was like a balloon, her eyes puffy slits—thank God for those ugly, heavily concealing glasses—and her hair... A small gasp of horror escaped her as she suddenly had a vivid and altogether revolting mental picture of her appearance. She hadn't been near a mirror in weeks, and the last time Sister Beatrice had tried washing her hair to make her feel more comfortable Sister Magda had come to their aid with a pair of surgical scissors. Her hand crept up to her clumsily cropped hair...she had actually begged Sister Magda to hack off a bit more, the bliss of losing that heavy, shoulder-length auburn curtain had been so great!

'I was just telling your husband that one of our offices is at your disposal.' The Ambassador's words cut across Sophie's thoughts, bringing her a merciful relief from them. 'No doubt you'd like to be alone while we await the military escort to the airport.'

'That's most kind of you, but it really isn't——' Sophie's blurted words came to an abrupt halt as her newly acquired husband grasped her by the arm, his fingers biting warningly into her flesh.

'We neither of us can find the words to thank you,' stated Patrick Carlisle, his formal words accompanied by an equally formal bow in the direction of the diplomat, before marching Sophie hurriedly from the room.

'Where are we going?' she gasped, almost stumbling in her attempts to keep up with him.

'As the Ambassador so romantically put it, you and I need to be alone,' he informed her brusquely, his long strides if anything lengthening. 'Without actually saying so, he's made it plain that it was only his sympathy for your plight that made him consent to the marriage being allowed in the first place,' he continued, virtually hauling her through a door and into a large, incongruously ornate office. 'But he made a few very pertinent points, which all lead to the fact that it's imperative we make sure our stories tally.'

'I don't understand,' protested Sophie, wondering when all this was going to end as she was impatiently pushed towards a dainty gilt chair in front of a huge carved desk.

'Something which is causing the Ambassador more than a little concern,' observed Patrick Carlisle wryly, hoisting his tall, lean frame on to the desk top as those shrewd green eyes lazily inspected her. 'Look, the militia—or whatever this rabble calls itself—could be here at any moment, so we haven't much time.'

Sophie moved uncomfortably on the high-backed chair. 'I'd like to take just a few moments of that time to thank you for——'

'Forget it—I just happened to be the only Spanish passport holder available,' he cut in, his smile doing much to temper the brusqueness of his words.

'But why a Spanish passport? I thought you were Irish.'

'I am—half. It's just that my mother's Spanish and I was born in Spain. Anyway, where was I? Just in case we're questioned ...' He hesitated, frowning. 'Hell, I've forgotten your name!' he exclaimed.

'Sophie—Sophie Drysdale.'

'God, you're almost as useless as I am at this,' he said with a groaned laugh. 'You have to fix it in your mind your name is now Sophie *Carlisle*!' His face suddenly grew serious. 'Just in case some bright spark decides to check the immigration records and finds... Sophie, are you listening to me?' he demanded sharply, as her head drooped forward in sleepy exhaustion.

'I'm trying to,' she croaked, striving desperately to clear her throbbing head. 'I wish I could shake off this feeling that any moment now I'll wake up and find this was all a bad dream.'

She neither heard nor saw him move, he just seemed to materialise crouched beside her chair.

'Sophie, I realise you've been very ill,' he told her gently. 'But it's imperative that you're aware of what's going on ... you are aware that there's been a coup here, aren't you?'

Sophie nodded. 'The nuns told me ... the rebels raided and burned down the clinic stores ... and the office ... my passport was in the office safe ... all my clothes——'

'I know, the sisters who brought you here explained,' he interrupted, again with gentleness. 'Sophie, it's important that you understand the political delicacy of what you've accidently become embroiled in. For reasons far too convoluted for me to be able to explain just now, it's essential that this embassy remains operative ... the rebels closed down the other embassies last week and expelled their staffs.'

'It comes as something of a surprise to me to learn that a tiny place like Gamborra runs to a Spanish Embassy, let alone others,' she muttered dazedly.

'That's understandable, given that one needs a pretty powerful magnifying glass to find it—even on quite detailed maps of Central Africa,' he said with a chuckle, suddenly rising to his full height. 'But what concerns us right now is that if the worst comes to the worst we're on our own—the Embassy staff can't be seen to have been involved in anything which——'

'What do you mean—if the worst comes to the worst?' asked Sophie, fear reawakening in her despite her feelings of exhausted detachment.

'I mean that should they start looking closely and notice that details of my wife were only added to my passport today; that if they ask for our marriage certificate and again find today's date; that if they check the records and find that you arrived here as a single person and on a British passport——'

'I think that's enough to be going on with,' muttered Sophie despondently, her shoulders sagging visibly.

'Cheer up—judging by the riff-raff in their ranks, I'd be surprised if many of them can read.'

'But who are they?' exclaimed Sophie. 'Until the raid, the nuns found it impossible to believe the reports they were getting. They regard this as one of the most politically stable countries you could hope to find in Africa.'

Patrick Carlisle shrugged. 'That's something that's still puzzling quite a few knowledgeable heads. But it's also something we haven't the time to discuss right now. As the Ambassador rightly implied, we need to get our story straight between us.' He smiled encouragingly down at her. 'Then, should the need to tell it arise, we shouldn't have many problems. We'll keep it as simple as possible, OK?'

Sophie nodded in half-hearted agreement, doubting if there could be any story simple enough to sink into and be retained by her mind in its present state of almost total non-function.

'Right—how long have you been nursing here? Come to think of it, what possessed you to choose Gamborra in the first place? There's no aid programme I know of here.'

'I trained with a girl from here... it's a little complicated,' she answered wearily. In fact, the only real complication, she admitted to herself, was that her mind simply balked at the minimal effort required to string the necessary words together.

'No matter,' he declared dismissively. 'You wouldn't necessarily have had to give me a reason.' Had he been able to see past the dark lenses of the glasses, he would have realised he was being treated to a look of complete bewilderment. 'So—here's our story and with only a few more embellishments added to what I've already implied to the Embassy staff. Ready?'

Sophie nodded, an awareness creeping into her that made her wish she didn't feel so ghastly. It occurred to her that had she been her normal self she would have been more than a little intrigued by this man— not just because he had turned out to be every bit as physically attractive in the flesh as he had seemed in broadcasts, but mainly because he must rank as the most totally laid back person she had ever come across. Knowing absolutely nothing about her, he had listened to her tale—told in the main by the nuns who had brought her here—had discussed it briefly with his colleagues and, with a casualness that still took her breath away, had offered himself, literally, as a solution.

'We met a year ago, and ten months ago we got engaged. Only two figures to remember—one year and ten months.' He flashed her a smile that Sophie felt certain must have wrought havoc with many a feminine heart at other times.

She nodded again, this time an answering smile creeping to her lips.

'So let's think ... where could we have met? The trouble is, I'm always on the move.'

'We met in London at the Institute of Oriental and African Studies,' replied Sophie, with a chuckle of impish delight. 'I attended a lecture you gave there and afterwards I asked you for your autograph.'

He gave her a puzzled look, then a disbelieving grin broke over his features. 'I did give a lecture there last September and . . . don't tell me you were actually one of those autograph hunters!'

'No,' laughed Sophie. 'But Susie, the girl I was sharing digs with then, was. She's one of your most ardent fans! So I shan't have any problem remembering our alleged meeting.'

'Good. Now we'll add a bit of melodrama—if they get as far as questioning us this closely, we might as well give them their money's worth. My mother wouldn't let you darken her door, so to speak.' There was a decided gleam of laughter in his eyes.

'Why ever not?'

'How about because my mother regards me as the greatest thing since sliced bread and would consider no woman worthy of me?' he suggested, then shook his head. 'No, we'll make it because you're not Spanish . . . that at a pinch she'd have settled for an Irish girl, but——'

'But never an English rose,' giggled Sophie, her sense of fun suddenly asserting itself. One thing that definitely could be said about Patrick Carlisle was that he had a most refreshing knack of not taking life in the least seriously . . . something for which she should be thanking every lucky star there was!

'And to try to win her over, you agreed that we should part—for how long . . . a year? That leaves us with two lots of one year and one of ten months to remember, OK?'

Sophie nodded enthusiastically.

'So, you took off for here . . . and when I heard of the coup I leapt on my white charger and came to rescue you with my journalistic colleagues, assuming I must be on to something, hot on my heels.'

'You make it sound almost as though you all needed an excuse to be here,' murmured Sophie. 'Why *have* all the foreign Press people been asked to leave?'

He shrugged. 'We haven't—not directly. It's just that our flight out of here will be the last for some time. They tell us the airport will be closed—for a period they didn't specify—after it.' He rocked on his heels as he spoke, the slight movement of his body allowing sporadic shafts of brightness from the window behind him to fall across Sophie's upturned face. She quickly lowered her head as he continued. 'At least that's their story. But I've a feeling the brains behind this coup—whoever they are—aren't too happy at the idea of having a handful of the world's top foreign affairs reporters plus their crews on the doorstep.'

'Do you think that's why they suddenly billeted you all here at the Embassy?' asked Sophie, striving to giving the appearance of being alert while every part of her craved the release of sleep.

'We were herded here this morning allegedly for our own safety, which is a joke considering you couldn't meet a more friendly and hospitable person than the average Gamborran.' He moved abruptly from her line of vision as he spoke, his action bringing her hands to her eyes as she tried desperately to protect them from the sudden, unbearable glare. 'No, I think this— and their sudden interest in scrutinising our travel

documents before leaving—indicates just how closely
they want to keep tabs on—— Are you all right?'

In her haste to escape the light, Sophie had sent
her protective glasses flying. With one hand now
clamped to her eyes, she was scrabbling in silent desperation at her feet with the other, trying to find them.

'Here, I've got them,' he said quietly, the sound of
his voice close beside her.

'I'm sorry——' Her words broke off with a gasp
of alarm as she felt herself and the chair lift suddenly.

'It's OK, I'm just moving you out of the glare,' he
explained, catching her as her unbalanced body fell
forward against the firm solidity of his. 'My God,
you really are in a mess,' he remarked candidly, the
gentleness of his fingers, as they attempted to smooth
away the tears now streaming down her cheeks, a disconcerting contrast to his almost callous words.

'It's not nearly as bad as it looks,' said Sophie,
giving an embarrassed little laugh as she replaced the
glasses. 'In fact my eyes are OK—it's just that they
can't take any light.'

'That's hardly what I'd describe as OK,' he informed her, bringing another gasp from her as he
swung her up effortlessly in his arms. 'Don't panic,
I'm taking you to the sofa in the corner, it's nice and
dark over there.'

'I really am practically recovered,' insisted Sophie,
as she felt herself gently lowered and a cushion placed
beneath her head. The crippling exhaustion that kept
threatening to overwhelm her was not being dissipated by feelings of squirming embarrassment. 'I'll
be fine here on my own, honestly. You don't have
to...'

'You're not suggesting that I abandon my bride, mere minutes after the ceremony?' he murmured, the gentle mockery in his words only increasing Sophie's feelings of discomfort.

'Oh, heck!' she groaned. 'I feel dreadful about...you know, the only reason I'm so vague...that I haven't been able to express my thanks to you properly...it's just that I'm still doped up to the eyeballs.'

'I'd never have guessed,' he responded drily, dropping to the floor and settling himself cross-legged with an agile grace Sophie found a little surprising in a man his size. 'And you can stop thanking me. Unless the old order is returned to power pretty damn quick, the pair of us could be regretting your losing your passport for a lot longer than I'd originally anticipated.'

'I didn't lose my passport!' exclaimed Sophie indignantly. 'It was...what do you mean, anyway?'

'*El embajador* has made it quite plain—in his oh, so diplomatic way—that there can be no scuttling off to London for us and telling all. This marriage is going to have to be annulled without any whiff of it ever coming out. You were lucky to come across a man as decent as he is, because I've a feeling that if our somewhat unorthodox nuptials were used as an excuse for closing down this mission, his career as a diplomat would come to an abrupt end.'

'This is dreadful...just dreadful!' exclaimed Sophie guiltily, deciding Patrick Carlisle must be one of the most perplexing men she had ever encountered as he responded to her words with a dismissive shrug. And also one of the most rash, she told herself bewilderedly—he had offered to marry her with about as much thought as he might have given to helping an old lady across a road! She gave a small shake of her head, but the *Alice in Wonderland* atmosphere in which she seemed trapped remained disturbingly intact.

'It's up to us to make sure it isn't dreadful. So, how about our going over that story once more?'

'Only if you need to,' replied Sophie decisively, the possible repercussions for the Spanish diplomat crystallising her thoughts far more than any consideration of her own possible plight ever had. 'I shan't forget a word of it.'

'Fine. So now you can tell me how you managed to land yourself in this spot—I missed chunks of it when you arrived earlier.'

Sophie found herself having to stifle a positive flash of resentment at his words; he made it sound as though she had brought the whole thing on herself, she thought crossly, then immediately reminded herself that if it were not for him she could well have ended up stranded indefinitely in what she felt had possibilities of becoming a civil war—it was obvious, even to an outsider such as herself, how happy the Gamborran people had been under their overthrown government.

'There's not a lot to tell,' she replied diffidently. 'About a month ago I developed viral conjunctivitis.' As she uttered them, she was struck by the clinical blandness of her words—words that spoke nothing of the pain and moments of stark fear that had disrupted the gentle peace of her existence. Even with her medical background, she had been unprepared for the stomach-churning terror that accompanied any threat to organs as vitally important as the eyes. 'Sister Magda did everything she could to ease the discomfort. The clinic was well-stocked until the rebel soldiers——'

'Are you saying you didn't see a doctor?' he interrupted in obvious alarm.

'Sister Magda *is* a doctor, and a very competent one too. She also called in one of the doctors from the general hospital for a second opinion——'

'An eye specialist?'

'No,' she replied a trifle sharply, wishing he would let her get on with it instead of constantly interrupting. 'Being such a small country, Gamborra doesn't run to many resident specialists, and anyway, the government has an agreement with Zaire...at least, it did till this ghastly coup took place,' she finished unhappily. Only now was the tragic enormity of what had happened fully sinking in, she realised dejectedly.

'The moment you get to London you should head straight for the nearest hospital,' he stated firmly. 'I'd hate to put a damper on your estimation of your recovery, but, apart from the fact that you appear disorientated almost to the point of being comatose, have you looked in a mirror recently?'

'I *am* a trained nurse,' snapped Sophie, realising instantly that it was straightforward vanity causing her shrewish reaction to this, his second deflatingly negative reference to her appearance. 'After the stores were destroyed, the sisters were left with scarcely anything in the way of drugs. Sister Magda had wanted me moved to the general hospital...she only told me this morning about the harassment of the expatriate staff there by the soldiers and how they were forced to leave the country——'

'Yes, getting rid of the few expatriates here seems to have been a deliberate policy,' mused Patrick Carlisle. 'The usual hypocritical statements of shock and regret being issued by the regime once they were safely out of the way—mainly to appease the local population who weren't at all happy when they got to hear about what had happened.'

'The village chiefs were so disgusted that they've organised an around-the-clock guard on the clinic compound——'

'You were telling me about the sister wanting you moved,' he stated abruptly. 'What sort of medical treatment were you able to have when that proved impossible?'

'I was in quite a bit of pain, so Sister Magda felt she had no option but to keep me sedated. The only thing she had for my eyes was atropine . . . it's a drug that dilates the pupils and enforces rest because the eyes just can't take light. The effects should start wearing off in a few days.'

'Does it also cause the face to swell?' he asked tersely.

Sophie pulled a wry face—perhaps it was just as well she hadn't had a chance to look in a mirror, she obviously looked a sight. 'No—that's just a secondary infection. It would have cleared up in no time with antibiotics, had we had any. In fact, your Russian colleague kindly gave me some so, with a bit of luck, I should be looking fairly normal by the time I reach London.'

'Valery Turyanov's renowned for his hypochondria,' he said with a laugh. 'He could probably restock the sisters' supplies with what he carts around with him.'

Sophie once more found herself noticing the agile grace with which he moved as he rose to his feet and drew a chair over towards the sofa.

'But I still think a thorough medical going-over must be your first priority on arrival,' he stated, straddling the chair and dropping his chin to the darkly tanned arms he folded across the top of its back. He was frowning slightly as those startlingly attractive green-flecked eyes of his made their leisurely inspection of her.

'And don't worry, I'll get it,' murmured Sophie, her heart suddenly sinking as her drowsy thoughts of how altogether extraordinarily attractive this man was were replaced by a sudden and sharply forbidding image of her father. 'Unfortunately, my father just happens to be an ophthalmic surgeon.' Noticing the puzzlement her words immediately brought to his eyes, she continued hastily. 'What I mean is...I've a feeling the mere thought of my father's profession tended to haunt poor Sister Magda. I'm pretty sure it influenced her decision to send me home, because——' She broke off with a start as she heard a door open.

'Sorry to interrupt—could I have a word with you, Patrick?'

Though she could not see him from where she lay, Sophie recognised the softly accented voice of the Russian who had given her the antibiotics.

'How are you feeling?' asked Valery Turyanov, moving into her line of vision.

'Much better, thanks to you,' murmured Sophie gratefully. 'I was just telling Mr Carlisle——' What she had intended saying was drowned by the laughter erupting spontaneously from both men.

'I know familiarity is alleged to breed contempt,' choked Patrick Carlisle, rising. 'But I shan't consider any liberty taken if you call me Patrick! Do you think you could manage that, Mrs Carlisle?'

'Oh, heavens, I'm sorry!' exclaimed Sophie, convinced now that when the time came she was going to make some careless mistake that would have undoubtedly catastrophic results. 'I think the wisest thing would be if I tried to get a little sleep—it might help gather up a few of my scattered wits.'

'A good idea,' agreed Patrick promptly. 'I take it Fred and José have turned up,' he added, addressing the Russian whom he now joined. 'My film crew managed to slope off soon after we were brought here— which sent most of the embassy staff into apoplectic fits,' he told Sophie, with a boyishly wicked grin. 'Shame they missed the big event really, they'd have made a delightful pair of bridesmaids.' Still laughing in unabashed appreciation of his own joke, he followed the Russian to the door. 'Sweet dreams, Mrs Carlisle,' he called over his shoulder, leaving Sophie shaking her head in bewildered amusement as he closed the door behind him.

The fact that Patrick Carlisle had turned out to be what she could only describe as a delightful nutcase was something for which she should be eternally grateful, she thought drowsily. The glasses slipped unnoticed off the end of her nose as she snuggled sleepily against the cushion he had placed beneath her head. In his televised reports he very rarely smiled, let alone laughed as she had seen him just now...though the subjects on which he reported were not usually even remotely humorous.

As the sleep she so craved came to claim her, she was chuckling softly to herself. Poor Susie... she had teased her friend quite mercilessly over her crush on the attractive reporter. But she supposed she had to admit that Susie did have a point—Patrick Carlisle really was quite the dishiest thing on two legs...

CHAPTER TWO

SOPHIE turned away with a muttered protest as a gentle tapping on her shoulder began dragging her from the bliss of sleep.

'You must wake up, Sophie. The militia are here to escort us to the airport,' urged Valery Turyanov, handing her the glasses for which she immediately began groping as she sat up.

'Thanks.' She put them on, surprised by the presence of the Russian. 'I was dead to the world,' she apologised shyly. 'But it's good to hear we're on our way.'

'Yes...we're almost on our way,' muttered the man, helping her to her feet, the expression on his face slightly speculative as he watched her vain attempts to smooth the creases from her badly crumpled dress. 'The emigration formalities are being dealt with here—not at the airport.'

'By the soldiers instead of the airport officials?' asked Sophie, something in his tone dispelling the last vestiges of sleep from her mind.

The Russian nodded, but said nothing, motioning her instead to follow him.

'Where's Patrick?' she asked, uncertain as to why alarm bells should be jangling so loudly in her head as she followed him to the door.

'Patrick's crew hasn't turned up yet.'

Sophie put her hand on the man's arm as he reached for the doorknob. 'There's no point my trying to go through emigration procedures if Patrick isn't here,' she pointed out quietly.

'It's all right,' he reassured her. 'Their only in terest is in making sure every member of the journalistic corps is on that plane. They came and collected our documents a few hours ago—I'd guess to check them against their immigration records. And though the ink was barely dry on your entry into Patrick's passport when they came, they showed absolutely no interest when it was pointed out that a husband and wife were travelling on the same passport.'

'Well, he'd better show up soon, otherwise this morning's ceremony will have been a waste of time— a wife can't travel alone on her husband's passport,' said Sophie, injecting a false brightness into her tone in an attempt to shake off an oddly persistent sense of unease.

'Even if he doesn't show up, you won't have any problem leaving, I'm certain of it.'

'And you're pretty certain he won't be back,' she stated quietly, wondering at the sixth sense within her that had penetrated this gentle, concerned man's attempt at deception. 'Valery, don't you think you should tell me what's going on?'

He hesitated, his hand dropping from the doorknob. 'Patrick's crew has been picked up by the military authorities...we're not sure why, but we're milking every contact we have to find out...' He turned towards her, his normally smiling face lined with worry. 'There's no way Patrick would leave them in the lurch and he has whatever backing the rest of us can give while we're still here. But this won't affect you, Sophie.'

'Does the Ambassador know?' asked Sophie, her own calmness, given her ever-changing circumstances, mildly surprising her.

'He knows José and Fred are missing, and he was less than happy when he learned that—but he doesn't know Patrick's gone...at least, not yet.' With a wryly apologetic glance in her direction, Valery Turyanov opened the door.

And that was that, thought Sophie fatalistically, wondering, as she stepped past him, if her gentle companion had ever come across the tale of *Alice in Wonderland* in acquiring his fluent and idiomatic use of English. If he had, he might have an inkling of her present mental state—though Alice at her most beleaguered could never have felt quite as disorientated as Sophie did now, she told herself dejectedly. And it wasn't the Cheshire cat she kept seeing, it was the image of Patrick Carlisle's handsome, laughing features that occupied her mind, and they showed no sign of fading.

And it was that image that had remained more or less intact in her mind, even after the immediate shock of the moments that had followed and subsided to no more than numbed bewilderment.

Yet it had been a false image, she thought, bewilderment and resentment welling within her as she now witnessed that face once more in the flesh—a face that denied all knowledge of laughter in the grimness of its barely suppressed fury. She had every sympathy with his desire to help his friends, but little with his hot-headed arguing with the heavily armed guards who had returned him to the Embassy, and even less with his arrogant rudeness towards the two exceedingly polite officers delegated to deal with the emigration procedures.

'I told you, I'm not leaving this place until I know where my crew are,' he stated implacably, immediately switching to a vitriolic tirade in Spanish in response to the Ambassador's quiet comment in the same language.

'I'm afraid you have no choice, *señor*,' interrupted the diplomat, his face tight with anger as he pointedly switched to English. 'You and your wife have been cleared to leave and I suggest you and she now board the coach before the authorities decide to take you both into custody.'

The look to which Sophie was fleetingly subjected by the man now technically her husband was one of total dismissal.

'This has nothing to do with her,' he snapped. 'She can——'

'The Ambassador's right,' cut in Valery Turyanov quietly, catching the angry man firmly by the arm.

'Would you excuse us for a brief moment, Mr Ambassador?' joined in a second, American-accented voice.

Another face familiar to television viewers, thought Sophie as she glimpsed the man who had joined the Russian and now held Patrick's other arm . . . Gordon somebody? No, somebody Jordan, she mused with little interest, leaning wearily against the wall as the diplomat gave a frigid bow of assent, then left the room. This wasn't happening, she tried to convince herself as the voices of the three men rose and fell in argument. Any moment now she would wake in her tiny room at the clinic and Sister Beatrice . . .

'OK, let's hit the road, as they say.'

Dragging her mind with considerable difficulty from its comforting thoughts, Sophie gazed up at the tall figure before her, now picking up a scuffed leather duffel bag and slinging it over one broad shoulder.

'About time too,' she observed acidly—as this was no more than a ghastly dream, she might just as well say what she felt.

'And what, precisely, is that supposed to mean?' he snapped, grasping her roughly by the arm and more or less dragging her along beside him as he strode from the room.

'Any fool would realise that creating a scene is more likely to do your friends harm than good,' she retorted, annoyed to find herself having to run to keep pace with his long, angry strides. 'Would you mind letting go of me? I'm perfectly capable of walking unaided.'

'As this is a subject on which you know absolutely nothing, I suggest you keep your opinions to yourself,' he snarled, his grasp on her arm unaltered as he marched her out into painfully bright sunlight and across to the waiting coach.

With her hand clamping the glasses firmly in place as the tears streamed in violent reaction down her cheeks, Sophie clambered up the steps. It wasn't her fault his crew had gone off and got themselves into trouble, she told herself angrily, flopping down on to the nearest seat and giving a silent groan of resignation as he eased his long, lean body down on the seat beside hers.

'Here,' he muttered gruffly, passing her a snowy white handkerchief. 'You're not exactly presenting a picture of an ecstatic bride.'

Sophie took the handkerchief and scrubbed list-lessly at her cheeks. Unfortunately her mind had now decided to attempt functioning, and the fuzzy, garbled miscellany with which it was now presenting her filled her with growing alarm. 'Would you mind if I asked you something?' she began tentatively as the coach lurched off.

'Ask away.'

'Exactly why did you marry me?'

He turned his face towards hers, its expression one of utter disbelief as his cool green eyes flickered over her ravaged features.

'I was in such a daze when I arrived at the Embassy,' she stammered, his look unsettling her. 'Everyone kept talking about my lack of papers...' She looked at him pleadingly.

'You mean nobody fully explained why it was imperative you had papers?' he asked incredulously.

'No...yes...I mean, they kept saying I'd never get out of the country without a passport, but——' She broke off with a helpless shrug.

'But what?'

'They seemed so nice—the new regime's officers who came to the Embassy—even when you got so unpleasant...' The scowling look her companion flashed her brought her words to yet another halt.

'That's some dope the sisters have been pumping into you!' he exclaimed abruptly. 'I can assure you I don't make a habit of marrying any waif and stray who happens to cross my path. The fact is, a couple of days ago I had the misfortune to catch sight of a woman who had found herself in a position pretty much the same as yours when her bag was stolen.' His eyes shifted from hers to gaze through the window, an almost nervous movement. 'She was one of the Belgian doctors . . . let's just say, she wasn't a pretty sight.'

'What had happened to her?' demanded Sophie, something indefinable in his tone unnerving her.

'She'd been beaten—and badly.' He gave a small shake of his head as though attempting to rid it of its grim memories. 'Mind you, she hadn't helped matters by clouting her guard over the head with a chair and trying to make a run for it—though God only knows where she thought she'd run to.' He leapt to his feet as the coach shuddered to a halt. 'They'd obviously tried patching her up before taking her to the airport,' he told her, his eyes hooded and unreadable as he gazed down at her. 'But those of us who caught a glimpse of her aren't likely to forget the sight in any hurry . . . so there you have it. Come along,' he added, stretching out a hand to her as he stooped and gazed once more out of the window. 'It seems we're being given door-to-door service—and to our very own jumbo, no less.'

Sophie clung on to the the proffered hand as he reached for his bag and returned it to his shoulder—she needed something to cling to because her legs were threatening to give way under her.

'Why had they beaten her?' she asked, this time not bothering to object as she was propelled at high speed across the short stretch of tarmac and up the steps of the aircraft.

'Because they're paranoically suspicious of any expatriate they can't immediately pigeon-hole. Once the woman's papers turned up and showed she was exactly who she claimed to be, they couldn't wait to get shot of her—they certainly didn't want the Belgian government kicking up a political stink over one of their nationals being held——' He broke off as they entered the aircraft and were greeted by smiling stewardesses. 'Where do you want to sit? It looks as though we're the only group travelling.'

'I feel dreadful,' gasped Sophie, clasping her arms across her chest as her imagination ran riot, not only with lurid pictures of what might have befallen her had this man—now regarding her with positive alarm—not come to her rescue, but also with guilt at the thought of the anxiety he must be feeling on behalf of his two crew men.

'Hell, this is all I need!' he groaned and, for the second time that day, scooped Sophie up effortlessly in his arms.

Frantically holding her glasses in place with one hand and clutching at a solidly muscled shoulder with the other, she tried to blot from her mind the soft stream of Spanish pouring from the man carrying her—unmistakable oaths, no matter what their language—and reached the inevitable conclusion that one of them was not completely sane.

'Just sit back and relax,' he muttered, his dark hair mingling with the rich auburn of hers as he held her closely against him, manoeuvering her with painstaking care on to one of the seats. 'You can stretch out once we're airborne.'

'Patrick, I——'

'For God's sake, stop arguing!' he snapped, then was immediately filled with contrition. 'I'm sorry... what I meant was, try to hang on till this thing's taken off.'

Try to hang on? To what—her sanity? Speechless with bemusement, Sophie watched as he searched around in one of the lockers above.

'Here, this should make you feel more comfortable.'

She felt a small pillow wedged awkwardly behind her neck, then the stifling weight of a blanket being tucked tightly round her. The temperature outside the aircraft was way into the nineties, inside it was only a degree or two lower, she told herself weakly... and here she was, being muffled up to her ears in a blanket!

'Patrick, I——'

'Yes? How do you feel?' he demanded, his tone verging on aggressive.

'Hot!'

'Don't worry! I'll get Valery... just try to relax, I'll be back as soon as I can!'

Don't worry? The man was mad! She closed her eyes, her swathed body immobile as soft waves of disbelief washed over her. She heard the monotonous whine of the engines swell to a straining roar, then later above that a calm, unhurried voice through the intercom. But none of the sounds around her was able to distract her from the dogged determination of her own thoughts. She began recapping her day from the moment she had awoken, following it step by step till she reached the point of her present state of utter bewilderment. The fault was hers—she was reacting slowly; her powers of reason weren't functioning in any way normally, which was perfectly understandable, pointed out the nurse in her, given that circumstances had necessitated her being sedated for several days—the effects of which would take some time to wear off. And today's nightmarish trauma had done little to help her state of mind. The truth was,

Patrick Carlisle was probably a perfectly sane man—
it was merely her mental confusion making him appear
otherwise.

'Sophie?'

Her eyes flew open and up into the anxious gaze
of Valery Turyanov.

'Patrick says he's sorry you were left on your own
during take-off,' he said, taking the seat next to hers.
'But they got this thing off the ground quicker than
any of us expected.' He hesitated, his kindly eyes minutely examining her face. 'Is it a headache, or were
you feeling sick?'

'I...I beg your pardon?' she stammered, alarm now
filling her. First Patrick Carlisle and now this man—
there was obviously something noticeably wrong with
her! Her hands flew to her face...perhaps she had
broken out in some sort of rash!

'Patrick said you were taken very ill as you came
on board,' stated the Russian anxiously.

'He what?'

'He said you told him you were feeling ill.'

For several seconds, Sophie gazed at her companion in blank incomprehension, then a groan of
pure disbelief squeezed its way out of her. 'Oh, for
heaven's sake!' she exclaimed, casting aside the re-
stricting blanket. 'I told him I felt dreadful—as in
guilty—not *ill*! He'd just told me what happened to
the Belgian doctor and I realised how worried he must
be about his crew members...oh, heck!' She turned
in surprise as Valery Turyanov buried his face in his
hands, laughter racking his body. 'It's not funny,' she
wailed, disconcerted to find her own lips twitching in
response to the sheer abandonment of his mirth.

'It is if you know Patrick as well as I do,' he choked. 'He's leapt into the role of a panic-stricken husband as though to the manner born! I believe he's actually had words with the captain—probably ordered him to put his foot down, or whatever it is pilots do to make planes go faster.'

As the Russian doubled up once more, delighting in his own joke, Sophie began wrestling to undo her seatbelt. 'Now I really do feel dreadful!' she exclaimed. 'Where is he?'

'Up in the lounge, with the rest of them,' he chuckled, placing a restraining hand on her arm as she made to rise. 'You stay there, I'll get him—put him out of his misery.' He rose, laughter still rumbling from him. 'Though perhaps you'd like to join us all for a drink.'

Sophie shook her head. 'Thanks, but I'd better not while I'm on your antibiotics.' She glanced at her watch and grinned up at him. 'Though I'd be grateful if you could get a stewardess to bring me an orange juice to help wash the next dose down—I'm just about due for it.'

As the still chuckling Russian nodded and left, she leaned back against her seat, a small smile curving her lips. All right, so she still felt woozy and not in the least like herself—and would probably remain so for a couple of days—but that latest panic had been no more than a simple misunderstanding, she comforted herself...and she had been in danger of letting it grow out of all proportion! Soon she would be back in London, and back to normal. Her smile faltered, a frown furrowing her brow as the image of her father crept into her mind. If he ever got to hear of today's happenings . . . a small shudder went through her as she immediately stifled the mere thought.

'Here's the drink you wanted.'

Sophie gave a small start, her eyes flying open and up to the tall figure of Patrick Carlisle on whose handsome features was an expression of scowling discomfort. With a murmur of thanks, she took the drink, finding herself having to suppress a spontaneous grin as she recalled the Russian's chortling delight.

'I'm glad you think it's funny,' he growled, flinging himself down on the seat beside hers.

'I'm sorry,' she muttered, busying herself with taking one of the pills. 'I really *am* sorry,' she choked, as laughter threatened to overcome her. 'But I did try to explain earlier that, despite my ghastly appearance, I'm not on the verge of physical collapse.'

'I'm not sure I'd describe your appearance as ghastly,' he murmured, amusement suddenly softening his features while his eyes perused her with a lazy deliberation she found disconcerting. 'A little on the puffy side, perhaps—and I'd be lying if I said that get-up does anything for you—but, as my Donegal grandmother would say,' he continued, his tone deadpan as he laid on the Irish brogue with a trowel, 'you've a fine pair of child-bearing hips on you and that's what counts.'

Sophie took a hasty gulp of her drink—his sense of humour was a trifle off-beat, to say the least—and promptly choked.

'Relax, I was only joking,' he drawled, removing the glass from her hand, then slapping her vigorously on the back. 'I do believe you're blushing, Carlisle.'

She was, she realised with mortified confusion, and the man making her do so couldn't even remember her name! 'The name's Sophie,' she informed him abruptly, struggling to regain a modicum of composure as she ducked away from his pummelling hand. 'And anyway, what's brought about this sudden change of mood?'

His response was a chuckle, a soft rumbling sound that did absolutely nothing for her composure in that it inexplicably triggered off a memory of the sensuous thoroughness with which those now teasing lips had kissed her only hours before, and also of her own totally uninhibited response to that kiss.

'Now that's what I like to see in a wife—a complete tuning in to each nuance of her husband's every mood.' He returned the glare she flashed him with a look of blank innocence. 'The police managed to get a message through to Ed Jordan, the NBC man...Fred and José have been transferred into their custody.'

'Is that good news?'

'It's great news,' he replied, the teasing humour disappearing without trace from his features. 'Having seen what those devils had done to a woman——' He broke off with shrug, then leaned his head wearily back against the rest.

Sophie reached out and placed a hand on his arm. 'I must have seemed incredibly unsympathetic about your crew——'

'They're not just my crew—they're two of the closest friends I have,' he stated woodenly.

'It's just that, until you told me about the Belgian doctor, I'd no idea...I just hadn't understood,' she stammered, conscious of how completely inadequate her words must sound.

'No—but there are things it might help if you understood now,' he replied, tempering the sharpness of his somewhat enigmatic words by covering her hand with his. 'You see, the police, virtually to a man, have no sympathy whatever with the new regime. Their intention is to let Fred and José "escape" over the border into Zaire as soon as an opportunity arises.'

'But that's wonderful!' exclaimed Sophie.

'It will be wonderful only if and when that plan succeeds,' he informed her brusquely, releasing her hand as he stretched restlessly, then slumped back against the seat. 'I've discussed tactics with the others and we've decided to hedge our bets by giving the regime a sustained dose of the publicity they're so intent on shunning, till both men are safely out. When I left them, they were putting their heads together to decide what sort of slant we should give the publicity.'

Sophie gave him a diffident smile, trying her best to look a little knowledgeable. It all sounded indescribably complicated to her...not surprising, considering she knew barely any of the pertinent facts. And not surprising, either, as she seemed to be viewing most things through a haze of mental confusion.

'We'll be serving dinner in a few moments,' announced a smiling stewardess. 'Would you like yours here or with the others?'

'The lady will have hers here,' replied Patrick, without even bothering to consult Sophie. 'I'm not hungry.'

'Neither am I,' added Sophie, forcing a smile to her lips as resentment welled in her at his high-handed manner.

'You should eat something,' he protested, frowning.

'I'm not hungry. But had I been, I'd have eaten wherever I chose.'

'Stop being so damned touchy,' he drawled. 'It's not often a handful of passengers have an entire jumbo at their disposal, but that's the only reason the captain agreed to these cabin lights being kept so low. With your affliction, you'd have problems coping with the lighting in the lounge.'

'It's not an affliction, for heaven's sake!' she exclaimed angrily. 'If you'd bothered to explain——'

'Stop ranting, Carlisle—you're beginning to sound like a fishwife,' he interrupted in that same infuriating drawl.

'And stop calling me Carlisle!'

'But "Mrs" is so formal.' His tone now reflected boredom.

'Why don't you just join the others and leave me alone?' she snapped, horrified to hear the distraught edginess in her words. She had never believed herself capable of over-reacting so grossly to what was, after all, only relatively harmless teasing on his part. It only went to show exactly how low a state, both physically and mentally, she was in, she thought nervously. But no matter how drained and close to total exhaustion she felt, the fact was that she owed this infuriating man beside her much more than she would ever be able to repay. 'Look, I'm sorry... I'm behaving very badly.' And she was about to behave ten times worse, she thought in a sudden welter of panic; she was about to inflict the ultimate humiliation on herself by bursting into tears! 'If you make so much as one of your clever Dick remarks, I'll... oh, heck!' The tears broke free, racing in an unstoppable torrent down her cheeks. 'It must be those damned sedatives—I *never* cry!'

'You're making a stunningly good imitation of doing so now,' he observed coolly, bringing a bellow of outrage from her. 'Sophie, I'm sorry...I'm useless around weeping females.'

'I'm *not* a weeping female,' she sobbed unconvincingly, deciding that this had to be the most utterly mortifying experience of her entire life.

'Oh, well, if that's the case, my shoulder's available for you not to weep on,' he responded with deadpan civility.

'I'd only make it soggy,' she retorted, her careless spontaneity contradicting her every heated claim.

'Not if you used the handkerchief I gave you earlier,' he pointed out reasonably, though to Sophie's now paranoically sensitive mind there were traces of what she regarded as sadistic enjoyment beneath that reasonable tone.

She took the handkerchief from her pocket and dried her eyes, scrubbing angrily at her cheeks as she did so. 'If you had an ounce of decency—or even tact—in you, you'd go away and leave me alone. I'd rather not have an audience when I curl up and die of embarrassment.'

'I can't see what there is for you to be embarrassed about,' he said softly, reaching out and firmly drawing her head down against his shoulder. 'As you've already admitted yourself, you've been doped up to the eyeballs for some time, on top of which, today's been one hell of a day by any standards.'

There was something she found strangely calming in the firm pressure of the arm now encircling her. 'And it can't have been all that great a day for you

either.' she sighed, a pleasurable warmth filling her
at the solid feel of his shoulder beneath her cheek.
And he smelled good too, she decided, fresh and mas-
culine and . . . somehow wholesome. 'I'm glad your
friends are safely in the hands of the police . . . I'm
sure they'll be free soon.' Her words came out in an
almost breathless rush as his hand began a gentle
stroking movement against her cropped hair. It was
a gesture that increased the sensation of warmth in
her by several startling degrees, and which heightened
her feelings of pleasure to an extent that was now
making her feel decidedly uneasy.

'Oh, dear, oh, dear, oh, dear.' He chuckled, the
soft sound sending a warning jolt of excitement
coursing through her as he turned, cupping her face
in his hands.

There were so many messages to be read in the brilliant green eyes gazing down into hers . . . amusement,
bemusement, and a dancing gleam of excitement.

'Oh, dear, what?' she croaked, scarcely recognising
her own distorted tones.

'Do you really have to ask?' he demanded huskily,
one hand sliding downwards till it rested against her
throat, covering the small pulse beating wildly beneath it. 'You have to admit we came pretty close to
disgracing ourselves after the wedding ceremony.'

She could only nod, mesmerised by those eyes, the
soft lilt of his voice and by the power of the unfamiliar sensations bombarding her with their clamorous
demands.

'And I'm afraid we're in grave danger of thoroughly
disgracing ourselves any moment now,' he continued,
his breath catching on the words as his arms now
moved around her body while hers, in a movement

that was entirely unselfconscious, rose to encircle his neck.

The mouth that swiftly sought and found hers did so with that same probing intimacy that had shocked her into such sudden arousal before. They were complete strangers, for heaven's sake! protested her mind in an instant of prim outrage, before her body responded with virtually the same degree of reckless eagerness it had displayed earlier.

The unrestrained plunder of his lips, the exciting warmth of the arms encompassing her, awakened in her a hitherto dormant capacity for passion, draining her mind of all else save its own powerful intoxicant. She felt the impatient strength in the arms straining her nearer, and the growing demand in her own body to be held ever closer. And when she felt him try to draw from her, a groaned oath escaping the lips still bruising their message of hunger on hers, her arms tightened in protest and her mouth began imparting its own inciting message against his.

'This isn't strength of will,' he groaned. 'I think I've just pulverised one of my ribs on that damned arm-rest.' He moved his face from hers, his breath coming in jerky bursts that fanned softly against her neck as he dropped his head to her shoulder.

'Do you always have this effect on women?' she demanded disjointedly, her senses reeling from shock-waves of the power of what had swept through her. 'Or have I just gone completely out of my mind?' Even as she spoke, she could feel that alien, sensual softness in her—a need to lay her cheek against the thick tousled blackness of his hair, to allow her fingers to caress in its glossy darkness.

'No, I don't!' he exclaimed with a groaned laugh. 'I'm finding this every bit as disconcerting as you obviously are.' He lifted his head, grasping her gently by the shoulders as his eyes, now a smouldering darkness, held hers. 'I'd say that lust at first touch seems a pretty apt description of what you and I have just experienced.'

'Not to mention second touch,' she muttered, remembering the startling effects of their earlier embrace. 'Oh, hell, what am I saying?' she groaned.

'You're being honest,' he replied softly. 'Most women would balk at admitting to honest to goodness feelings of lust.'

'Considering the way I've just behaved, I've no option but honesty,' she declared miserably, then found her misery eased by the quite dazzling smile that danced its way across his features.

He was just about the most attractive man she had ever clapped eyes on, rationalised her mind as her stomach immediately launched into a series of most unsettling somersaults; added to which, he was blessed with more than a fair share of wit and intelligence. And she was an allegedly mature and level-headed twenty-three-year-old, pointed out a small unsympathetic voice inside her, not an impressionable teenager!

'Would you stop looking at me like that, Carlisle? We have a problem,' he objected huskily, his fingers tightening a fraction on her shoulders.

'Like what?' she demanded mechanically, trapped in a spell she could muster no will to break.

He gave an exaggerated sigh as, ignoring her words, he guided her body back against her seat, then leaned back in his own.

'Given our decidedly unique circumstances, I think it's best if I don't mince my words,' he began quietly. 'I think I should start by saying I have the same sexual appetites as have most other normal, healthy men——' He broke off as Sophie suddenly leaned forward and peered into his face. 'What?' he demanded impatiently.

'Nothing,' she murmured innocently, returning to her former position. 'It's just that I have difficulty working out exactly when you're joking. You were explaining about your normal, healthy sexual appetites.'

'I also happen to have an abnormally quick temper,' he growled, though there were positive undertones of amusement in his tone. 'What I was trying to explain, before your facetious interruption, was that I don't usually have much difficulty exercising control over such appetites...in fact, one or two women I've known have gone as far as to accuse me of being cold-blooded. Damn it, Sophie, I'm trying to have a serious conversation with you!' he exploded, as a choked giggle erupted from her.

'I'm sorry,' she protested weakly. 'But if it's any consolation, I've often had the same accusation levelled at me.'

'Frankly, it's no consolation,' he snapped. 'With the chemistry we have going between us, I doubt if——' He broke off with an exclamation of impatience. 'The point I'm trying to make—if you'd only let me—is that marriage is an institution I happen to regard with the utmost respect. I believe in its sanctity, and that it is a commitment two people make to one another for the rest of their lives.'

'But you married me without appearing to give it a second thought,' blurted out Sophie, sharp stabs of guilt swiftly killing off her earlier amusement.

'To be honest, I gave it several thoughts—not that this will count as a marriage, as it will be annulled as soon as it possibly can be, thank God.' He turned and glared at her. 'Would you kindly stop interrupting me and let me get to the real point of what I'm trying to say?' he demanded. 'To put it bluntly, I didn't envisage this complication, but, were we to end up making love, I've a nasty feeling my conscience might choose to regard it as some sort of consummation of the marriage—no matter what the initial reasons for its having taken place... Does that make any sense whatever to you?' he demanded with a groan of exasperation patently directed towards himself.

'Patrick, I promise you, I understand exactly what you mean,' she assured him earnestly, realising just how much about his integrity his words had unwittingly revealed—not to mention how horribly trapped he felt by the farcical marriage into which that same integrity had pushed him. 'But it's hardly a problem that's ever likely to arise again once we're back in England and out of each other's lives.'

'I only hope it will be that simple,' he sighed morosely, rising from his seat. 'I suppose I ought to go and find out what the others have come up with.' There was a coolness in the eyes that flicked over her that Sophie found disturbing, given the turbulent memories suddenly crowding back into her mind. 'You'd better get some sleep,' he told her. 'I arranged for a message to be radioed through to your father

to be at the airport, so we can't have you looking——'

'You what?' she gasped, every nerve in her body
freezing in protest.

'While I was still under the impression you were on
the verge of collapse, I spoke to the captain,' he stated,
his eyes narrowing in puzzlement.

'But I'm *not* on the verge of collapse!' she wailed.
'My father's the last person I want to see!'

'Don't be silly!' he exclaimed coldly, his expression
openly impatient. 'You have a problem with your eyes,
and you did say he was an ophthalmic surgeon, didn't
you?'

'Yes, but . . . you're right,' she capitulated wearily,
'I'd best get some sleep.' She closed her eyes, wishing
she could close her mind to the images leaping into
it of her forthcoming confrontation with her father.

CHAPTER THREE

'For God's sake stop behaving like a spoiled brat!' exclaimed Patrick Carlisle, scowling at Sophie as the two of them entered the Customs hall a good way behind their travelling companions. 'How was I supposed to know you were conducting some sort of petty feud with your father? Do you want me to go ahead and explain things to him?'

'I am *not* a spoiled brat,' retorted Sophie, her blood dangerously near to boiling-point. 'I am *not* conducting a petty feud with my father. And there is *nothing* you can explain to him. I've already told you—he didn't want me to go to Gamborra in the first place, and anything that has happened to me during my stay there he will consider to be entirely my own fault.'

'Of course he can't blame you for—— Oh, for God's sake, this is bloody ridiculous!' he exploded. 'Stay here. Give me five minutes with him, then come out.'

'I've told you——'

'And I've told you!' he snapped. 'For once in your life, do as you're damn well told! Five minutes,' he reiterated threateningly, then strode to the exit leaving Sophie alone and feeling curiously vulnerable without his hectoring presence.

She should never have mentioned it to him, she berated herself bitterly, giving a sudden start as one of the Customs officials approached her.

'You can go straight through, miss.'

'Thanks,' she muttered self-consciously, her steps dragging visibly as she slowly made her way towards the exit. So much for Patrick's five minutes, she told herself wryly—now she would have both him and her father nagging at her. To hell with the pair of them, she decided and, with a defiant toss of her head, marched through.

It was the tall, elegant figure of her mother that she first spotted—standing beside the figures of her father and Patrick, deep in conversation. She watched, her steps growing less confident, as her mother caught sight of her and ran to her side.

'Darling, thank God you're safe and reasonably sound!' exclaimed Elizabeth Drysdale, her eyes brimming with tears as she hugged her daughter.

'I'm sorry you've been dragged out here at this hour, Mummy,' choked Sophie, genuine tears inexplicably mingling with those already streaming down her cheeks in protest against the light penetrating her dark glasses. 'It was a complete misunderstanding that made Patrick have that message sent out for Daddy. I didn't mean to worry you.'

'Of course we were worried, darling,' choked her mother, giving her another hug before stepping back to examine her. 'My, you have been in the wars,' she sighed. 'But your father can give you a thorough going-over.'

'I suppose he's furious,' muttered Sophie, her streaming eyes flicking towards the two still engrossed men.

'Darling, of course he's not. He's been worried ever since we heard of this wretched coup,' protested her mother. 'His only concern right now is for your well-being.'

'Until he hears about the marriage,' sighed Sophie. 'Then all hell will be let loose . . . I'd better explain to you.'

'The young man already has,' Elizabeth Drysdale informed her, amusement curving her lips. 'And your father, believe it or not, has taken it remarkably calmly.' She linked her arm in Sophie's as she glanced over at the men. 'You know, his face seems somehow familiar—have I met him before?'

The remark was so typical of her mother, it brought a smile to Sophie's lips. 'No,' she chuckled. 'You've probably seen him on television, though I'm amazed you've ever found time to watch it. How's the new research unit going?'

'How can you ask me about my work at a time like this?' demanded Elizabeth Drysdale, to her daughter's complete amazement—a gifted renal consultant, her mother generally lived and breathed her work. 'Good, they've spotted us!' she exclaimed, as the two men looked up, then began walking towards them.

'So—the prodigal daughter returns,' murmured Charles Drysdale, a smile tinged with exasperation on his patrician features as he opened his arms to his decidedly wary daughter.

'I was sure you'd be livid,' she admitted as she was swept into a paternal hug.

'I would be—if I weren't so damned worried about you,' he retorted gruffly, holding her from him and inspecting her.

'I'm fine—honestly.'

'I'll be the judge of that,' he informed her abruptly, removing her glasses and giving an exclamation of

disbelief at what he glimpsed before Sophie was able
to fling her arm across her violently protesting eyes.
'I think we'd best get you straight to my consulting-
rooms,' he stated briskly, placing the glasses back on
her, his overcoat round her shoulders and a firm arm
around her on top of it.

Her face burrowed against her father, Sophie could
almost feel her mind switching off as exhaustion, both
physical and mental, finally caught up with her. The
sounds of her mother's and Patrick's voices drifted
meaninglessly in her ears. Then it was just her father's
voice, probing and insistent as he questioned her in
exhaustively meticulous detail about her eyes.

It was only when she and her father stepped from
the taxi outside his consulting-rooms that the fact
slowly registered with her that they had travelled alone.

'Why aren't we using your car?' she exclaimed
dazedly. 'Where's Patrick . . . and Mummy?'

'Your mother's taken Patrick to fetch his car—in
mine,' replied her father, fumbling for a moment with
keys, then leading her inside.

'Why couldn't we have gone with them?' protested
Sophie querulously—her head was splitting, her legs
felt like jelly and all she wanted to do was sleep.

'I want to give you a thorough going-over. For all
I know, that damned nun could have botched your
eyes for good,' he replied with his customary candour.
'And besides, your mother and I are supposed to be
driving up to Scotland for a spot of fishing with the
Fergusons this afternoon—first time in months she
and I have had a couple of weeks off that coincide.'

'I told you—I'm fine,' she protested wearily as she
was led into a magnificently equipped examination-
room.

'I hope so—I'm looking forward to Scotland,' murmured Charles Drysdale. 'Now—up you get on that stool, and place your chin on the support. And just do as you're told.'

Despite feeling near to collapse from exhaustion, Sophie felt those words strike an all too familiar chord in her. 'You and Patrick Carlisle should get on like a house on fire,' she muttered rebelliously as she climbed on to the stool. 'He's also very practised at dishing out orders to others.'

'He seems a most likeable and intelligent young man,' stated her father, uncharacteristically not rising to the bait. 'We'll discuss him later, but for now I want you to do *precisely* as I tell you for the next half an hour or so.'

It was well over half an hour—in fact, nearer an hour of barked instructions and being observed through all sorts of gadgetry before her father finally switched off the machines and went to wash his hands, by which time, almost comatose from tiredness, Sophie was barely capable of registering surprise when she heard her mother's softly anxious tones.

'Stop fretting, Lizzie, there's no real damage,' murmured Charles Drysdale briskly.

It was not her father's words, but the sound of Patrick Carlisle's voice from directly behind her that made Sophie start and almost fall from the stool.

'That was quite some examination—how do you feel?'

'Fine,' she replied, her response purely reflex as, with her head swimming with a mixture of bewilderment and weariness, she climbed down from the stool and gazed blankly first at her mother, then at the tall figure of the man beside her.

'There's a fair bit of corneal scarring,' announced her father, returning to Sophie's side and giving her cheek an encouraging pat. 'Especially to the left eye— but that will fade with time.' He tilted her face up towards his. 'You'll also experience photosensitivity for a few weeks, because of that damned atropine.'

'Sister Magda had no choice but to use it,' said Sophie defensively, her mind giving up its half-hearted attempts to puzzle out why and when her mother and Patrick had appeared on the scene.

'I realise that, poppet,' placated her father, slipping his arm round her. 'In fact, your Sister Magda did all she possibly could, given the circumstances—a fine job.' He turned to Patrick. 'So, young Carlisle, she's all yours.'

By the time his words had meandered their way into Sophie's minimally functioning mind and begun eliciting the stirrings of protest, her train of thought was disrupted by her mother's voice.

'Charles, I really think we ought to postpone leaving——'

'So would I if I had the slightest doubt over Sophie's prognosis,' cut in her husband. 'But I haven't, and I think Patrick's perfectly capable of administering what little medication she'll need.'

Sophie shrugged free from her father's arm, an expression of bewildered outrage on her face as she strove to make a semblance of sense of what she was hearing.

'Would you mind not talking about me as though I weren't here?' she objected. 'I don't need Patrick or anyone else, I'm perfectly capable of taking care of myself!'

'I take it you haven't discussed this with her!' exclaimed Patrick, exasperation in his expression as he glanced questioningly at the man beside him.

'I was going to bring it up once I'd finished examining her——'

'Bring *what* up?' beseeched Sophie, turning to her mother.

As both her parents began speaking in unison, it was Patrick Carlisle's authoritative tones that immediately overrode them.

'It was decided that, as my crew are hardly household names, the only way to publicise their plight would be to do so through me. The tabloids enjoy nothing more than a wedding, so that's what we'll give them. It won't take much in the way of manipulation to have them wallowing in whatever sentimental claptrap we choose to feed them... such as the one dark cloud on our blissful horizon being the plight of the groom's closest friends.'

'I thought the idea was to get this marriage annulled as quickly and as discreetly as possible, not splash it across headlines,' croaked Sophie, her beleaguered mind resorting to its now familiar ploy of promising that soon she would wake from this exhausting, confusing dream.

'It was,' snapped Patrick. 'But my exclusive concern right now is the well-being of two men I regard almost as brothers, and if by splashing news of the marriage across every headline from here to Timbuktu I can help them, I'll consider it worth any resulting hassle.'

'Darling, you owe it to Patrick,' pointed out her mother quietly. 'If it hadn't been for his selfless action in——'

'I *know* what I owe Patrick!' exclaimed Sophie wearily. 'And I'm quite prepared to do whatever I can to help...I'd just find life a little less confusing if people took the trouble to let me in on what was going on, that's all!'

Sophie woke with a muffled reflex groan in response to the sound of a sharp rap on the door. She sat up with a start, her mind, in its instant of waking, a complete blank.

'It's time you woke up—you'll never sleep tonight,' came Patrick Carlisle's softly accented tones, jolting awareness back into her groping mind with the sound of his voice and the sight of his tall, well-built body silhouetted by a distant light as he approached the bed. 'Besides, it's time you started getting some of these drops into you,' he added, reaching out and snapping on the bedside lamp.

As the soft glow filled the room, Sophie heard the sharp intake of his breath almost in the same instant she became aware of her own nakedness.

'What drops?' she muttered, dragging the duvet up over her exposed breasts, acutely conscious of his eyes on her and her undeniable feelings of pleasure at the sight of the open appreciation evident in them.

'These,' he announced, waving a bottle under her nose. 'Your father says you're to have two drops in each eye every four hours.' He sat on the bed and handed her the bottle. 'He also says you're to keep taking Valery's antibiotics—I'll get you some water for that while you bung in the drops.'

'This is ridiculous,' she groaned. 'Absolutely, completely and utterly ridiculous!'

'There's no need to throw a fit,' he informed her tersely. 'If you can't manage the drops on your own I'm perfectly capable of giving you a hand.'

'I didn't mean the drops!' she exclaimed. 'I meant...oh, heck, I'm not in the least sure what I meant,' she finished with a hopeless shrug that necessitated her grabbing the duvet to her once more.

'I've a pretty good idea what you meant, Carlisle,' he sighed morosely. 'But like it or not, we're saddled with this bloody set-up...so, do you need a hand or don't you?'

'I need a hand.'

'Right—head back and eyes open wide.'

'Why do you keep calling me Carlisle?' she asked as he painstakingly inserted the drops.

'Why not?' he muttered non-committally, replacing the stopper in the bottle.

'I think it's because you have problems remembering my name.'

'Of course I don't have problems remembering your name, Clementine, it's just that Carlisle suits you better,' he retorted, placing the bottle on the bedside table.

'And "Mrs" is so formal,' she said with a chuckle, screwing her eyes tightly shut as the drops began stinging sharply.

'Are you all right? Is that supposed to happen?' he demanded in alarm.

'Stop panicking, it just stings a bit,' she explained. 'You know, I really don't think you're cut out for this—nurses are supposed to remain cool, calm and collected at all times.'

'The way you do?' he asked innocently, rising. 'Just for that, you can get up and fetch your own water.'

He sauntered towards the door. 'Until you sort through your own things, you'd best put this on,' he told her, taking a dressing-gown from the back of the door and flinging it over to her. 'And, for the sake of my blood-pressure, I think we should set about establishing a few house rules pretty damned quickly.'

His soft laughter seemed to dance in the air for several seconds after the door had closed behind him as Sophie slipped out of bed and into the dressing-gown. She was conscious of the mild battle taking place inside her as she tried, with no success, to ignore the acute awareness tingling in her with a sharpness that verged on excitement. She wrapped the robe—obviously Patrick's and therefore massive—around her and belted it securely. Then she sat down on the edge of the bed, a deep frown of concentration furrowing her brow.

It was time she faced facts and stopped kidding herself this was all a dream, she told herself firmly. And she could also dispense with blaming possible side effects of Sister Magda's sedatives on her disconcerting physical response every time Patrick Carlisle so much as laid a finger on her! The man had married her in the reasonable assumption their return to England would bring about a swift annulment of the marriage. That circumstances now dictated otherwise, he was now finding an obvious strain—more so, undoubtedly, because of the strong sexual attraction now exacerbating an already contentious situation. The restless excitement she was experiencing should be a warning of the danger inherent in attempting to minimise the strength of that attraction, and the futility of denying that there was something very much over and beyond his extravagantly good looks that was attracting her...that was allowing him to get under her skin in a way no other man ever had.

She rose, her frown deepening. The plain truth was that, in normal circumstances, he would probably have never even given her a second look—certainly not with her looking as ghastly as she did now.

It was vanity, pure and simple, that drew her to the dressing-table mirror and drove her to examine minutely her appearance. At least the swelling had all but gone down—but her hair looked a positive mess, she thought dejectedly, impatiently dragging her fingers through its still unfamiliar cropped shortness.

'Sophie? You haven't gone back to sleep, have you?'

'No—I'm coming,' she called, giving her re flection one last dissatisfied look before donning the loathsome, unflattering glasses and making her way out into the hall.

'Where are you?' she called, opening a door before her and finding another bedroom—this one much larger than the one she had been in, and with most of the contents of Patrick's half-emptied duffel bag strewn in a jumble across the huge bed dominating it.

'Come on, I'll show you around,' he offered from behind her, making her start guiltily.

His idea of showing her around comprised his pointing in the direction of closed doors and stating what lay behind them, apart from the one room into which he led her: the kitchen—an airy, gleaming and lavishly equipped place of the variety more usually adorning the pages of glossy magazines than actual homes.

'I'd no idea you'd be this domesticated!' she ex
claimed, her eyes skimming round the myriad built-
in, hi-tech pieces of equipment.

'Actually, the only things I've ever been able to
fathom how to use are the washing-machine, the drier
and the cooker,' he informed her without the slightest
trace of embarrassment.

'Why on earth have you so much gadgetry if you
don't know how to use it?' gasped Sophie.

'It came with the place,' he explained. 'I told the
estate agent's I wanted something functional—
meaning somewhere I could sleep and work—and they
seemed to think that meant a space-age kitchen. Can
you cook?'

'Yes,' laughed Sophie. 'Can you?'

He shrugged, seeming suddenly bigger and taller as
he gazed teasingly down at her. 'I tend to eat out...but
I can cook if required to. In fact, I got some food in
this afternoon.'

Sophie gazed up at him, puzzled. 'What time is it?'

'Six-thirty.' He grinned.

'I don't believe it!' she groaned. 'How could you
have let me sleep so long?'

'Your father insisted you weren't woken—when he
and your mother brought round the drops and your
things.'

'Brought round my things? You mean they're on
their way to Scotland already?' she wailed.

'It's funny—this morning you were carrying on like
one demented at the mere thought of seeing your
father,' he murmured innocently. 'And now you're
carrying on like one abandoned because he's no longer
here.'

'I'm *not* carrying on,' she snapped, irritated more with herself because she knew how completely irrational her behaviour must seem…was. 'May I have a glass? I'd like to take my pill.'

'You may—top left-hand cupboard behind you. And don't go all prissy on me, Carlisle, or I'll not cook your supper!'

Against her will she felt laughter bubbling in her as she found a glass, filled it and took her pill.

'So, what were you planning on cooking?' she asked, unable to suppress her amusement. 'I'm starving.'

'Well, there's plenty of bread and cheese.' He pulled a long-suffering face as hers registered disappointment. 'Oh, all right, then, I'll do you an omelette,' he muttered ungraciously, opening a cupboard and taking out a heavy cast-iron pan. 'You get the plates and cutlery out; we'll eat in here,' he added, indicating an alcove at the far end of the room.

'Where do you keep everything?' she asked, watching with stirrings of alarm as he poured what seemed like the best part of a litre of green-tinged olive-oil into the pan.

'Just poke around in the cupboards, you'll soon find things,' he muttered vaguely, his concentration engaged by the several knobs he seemed to be fiddling with at random.

When, still twisting knobs and pushing buttons, he began muttering softly in Spanish under his breath, it suddenly dawned on Sophie just how minimal his familiarity with the cooker was. As his mutterings took on a somewhat savage note, Sophie yanked open the cupboard nearest her and put her head in it, frantically trying to stifle her laughter. When she felt sufficiently in control to emerge, it was to find him flinging several cloves of unpeeled garlic into the lake of olive-oil.

'I thought you said you were doing omelettes,' she choked, her control all but deserting her.

'I'm doing them the Spanish way,' he informed her tersely.

'Do you always use that much oil?' she asked, her face aching from the strain of trying to keep it straight.

'I thought I'd make one big one,' he muttered uncertainly. 'Hell, I was banking on your offering to do it—most women do!' he exclaimed, alarm on his face as the oil began smoking ominously.

'My God, you're absolutely pathetic!' she retorted, shoving him aside and removing the pan from the heat. 'Why couldn't you just admit you can't cook?'

'I can—sort of. It's just that I seem to be the only person I know capable of stomaching the results.' He grinned shamelessly. 'Perhaps it would be better if we just swopped chores.'

'All I can say is that your women deserve you if they're stupid enough to fall for that routine,' said Sophie. 'I hope you have some butter... and do you really want all that garlic in your omelette?'

'Do what you like, Carlisle—your masterfulness impresses me,' he murmured, batting his eyelids outrageously at her before fetching butter from the fridge. 'Perhaps you could tackle the mysteries of the dishwasher later—none of my other women ever cracked that particular puzzle, though, to give them their due, I have misplaced its instructions... plus all the others.'

Though there were several times when she found his teasing banter, and what she was certain was his deliberately exaggerated domestic cluelessness, exas-

perating as she cooked and served the meal, deep
down she had to admit how thoroughly she was en-
joying his madcap company—his lazy charm, his ef-
fortless wit and, perhaps most of all, his sheer
unpredictability.

'You get yourself off into the living-room and I'll
bring in the coffee,' he announced when they had finished eating. 'You can work out the mysteries of the
dishwasher and tackle the washing-up later,' he added
with a cherubic smile.

'I take back what I said earlier—no woman could
ever deserve the likes of you, Carlisle,' she declared,
rising and padding barefoot across the tiled floor.

With his laughter still rumbling in her ears, she
entered the living-room, a dreamy smile of contentment on her lips as she tried each of the several lamps
in the large, elegantly furnished room until she found
one that gave out only the gentlest of glows. Appre-
hensively she removed the glasses, heaving a sigh of
relief as her eyes scarcely reacted. Then she went to
the three tall Georgian windows and drew their heavy,
rich green velvet curtains, feeling oddly like a small
child revelling in playing house.

'I take it this dimness is to accommodate your eyes,
not part of a plan for my imminent seduction,' he
teased as he entered and strolled across the room to
place a tray on a large, low coffee-table. 'How about
something with this—cognac, or a liqueur?'

Annoyed by the hot colour his joking words had
brought rushing to her cheeks, Sophie shook her head,
busying herself unnecessarily with the curtains. 'I'd
better not, with the antibiotics.'

'Well, stop being so damned domesticated and come
and sit down. How do you want this—black or white?'

'White, please.'

He glanced up as she seated herself on the large cushioned sofa, his expression quizzical. 'Is it my imagination, or are Papa's drops already working wonders?' He abandoned the coffee and came to her side, taking her chin in his hand. 'Why, I do declare, Carlisle—apart from the odd bloodshot speck here and there, you have a pair of the biggest, most stunning blue eyes I've ever seen!'

'It's probably the antibiotic helping too,' she muttered uncomfortably, finding herself incapable of matching his teasing tone as she fretted over whether the sudden and thunderous increase in her heart-rate was manifesting itself visibly against the fabric of the dressing-gown. 'I think there might have been a bit of secondary infection in both my eyes,' she babbled, determined to distract him from the material she felt certain was heaving as though suddenly imbued with a life of its own. 'You see, antibiotics can't help viral infections——' She broke off, horrified by the panic she heard creeping into her tone.

'You don't say,' he murmured, a slight huskiness distorting those teasing words. 'Sophie, we never did get round to those house rules I mentioned earlier,' he added, his hand suddenly tilting her chin till she had no option but to look into his eyes.

What she saw there sent a small shiver of apprehensive excitement running through her, and even as he bent his head to hers she could feel her mouth part in trembling anticipation of the turmoil of pleasure his would bring. She felt the tremor that rippled through him as his hands slipped past the collar of the robe, warm and impatient against her skin as they drew her against him. And in the bruising exploration of the mouth now claiming hers was that same intoxicating madness with which his touch had first filled her and which now she had unconsciously sought as though it were a drug to which she were now addicted.

There was no thought of struggle in her mind as he drew her down on the sofa, holding her fiercely against the length of him as his lips searched in growing hunger against hers, inflaming her with their ardent message till her response more than equalled the passion of his.

'Sophie, I don't want to stop,' he groaned incoherently, his hands moving against her shoulders as though to drag the robe from them. 'Please . . . please help me stop!'

It was the note of alarm in those pleading words that penetrated the shroud of madness blocking her ability to reason, bringing her to her startled senses with a sudden surge of panic in which she pushed him violently from her.

He landed on the floor with an almighty thud and a yell of startled indignation.

'Patrick, I'm sorry! I didn't mean...are you hurt?' she babbled, leaping up and rushing to his prone figure.

'Just don't come near me!' he exclaimed, rising gingerly and studiedly brushing himself down before flinging himself on to one of the armchairs. 'This is lunacy...sheer, unadulterated lunacy!' he pronounced disjointedly, glaring accusingly at her as she returned to the sofa, her mind reeling with disbelief and self-recrimination while her body still clung tenaciously to the lingering aftermath of the sensations so recently bombarding it. 'And for God's sake don't start getting uptight on me—I've enough on my plate without having that to contend with.'

'*You've* enough on *your* plate?' she burst out angrily, her words distorted and breathless. 'Yes . . . I suppose you have,' she sighed, her mood lurching from outrage to dejection in a manner she found most alarming. 'But I can assure you, uptight is hardly the word for the way I feel.'

'Well, whatever the word is, it no doubt describes feelings that are completely mutual,' he snapped, his eyes enigmatic slits as they watched her. 'And, at the risk of stating the obvious, I'd say it would pay us to keep firmly in mind how devastating a force sexual chemistry can be.'

But a force she had always believed would only manifest itself in her with a man she loved, she told herself indignantly, not with the indiscriminate, almost animal suddenness with which it had shattered her entire equilibrium in the arms of this man . . . this stranger who openly resented her enforced presence in his life and the strength of their disconcerting mutual attraction. Yet with him she seemed to have absolutely no control over feelings of such raw sexuality that they shocked her profoundly.

'Is it really necessary for me to stay here?' she pleaded miserably, escape the only possible solution beckoning her.

'Once the story breaks the Press would have an even bigger field day if you didn't.' He shifted suddenly in his chair. 'Obviously you'll have to stay here. And there's little point in either of us sinking into the depths of depression over that fact,' he added with unremitting candour, before managing the ghost of a smile. 'I mean, it isn't as though either of us is the type to go leaping on unsuspecting members of the opposite sex like a rapacious maniac, now, is it?'

Her eyes rose to his, wariness accentuating the tense pallor of her features. 'You may joke about it, but nothing alters the resentment you must feel at the way I've disrupted your life.'

'I always have the thought of the publicity the marriage can generate with which to console myself,' he replied, not even attempting to deny her statement. 'It could well turn out that you'll be doing me a favour every bit as important as the one I did you ... so feel free to remind me of that fact, should the need arise.' He flashed her a sudden grin. 'And as for the joking, you have to admit that, from a male point of view at least, there's a somewhat macabre humour in a man not daring to lay a finger on a woman he desires intensely, for the sole reason that he's married to her.'

'I'd say that probably makes you unique among men,' managed Sophie, startled by the casual candour with which he referred to the strength of his feelings towards her, and wondering if she would ever become accustomed to his lightning mood changes as he suddenly adopted an expression of doleful suffering which swiftly deteriorated into a teasing grin.

'Now that we're agreed on my uniqueness—how about your showing a bit of community spirit and pouring the coffee?' he murmured with studied innocence. 'That noble and monumental display of willpower has left me in a state of total exhaustion.'

'I see you're an avid believer in giving credit where it's due,' she admonished with a laugh, rising and pouring the coffee.

'Will you always be the one due the credit?' he demanded softly.

'I wouldn't bet on it if I were you,' she responded without thinking, and immediately felt warm colour rushing to her cheeks. 'When is the story of the marriage likely to break?' she asked, swiftly changing the subject.

'OK, I'll let you off the hook—this time,' he murmured, his eyes sweeping down her in a manner that immediately started up the now familiar churning sensation in the pit of her stomach as she handed him a cup. 'This is something I suppose we really should discuss. The marriage will have to be announced tomorrow. We delayed it on the off chance there might be good news from our Gamborran contact—there's been none.'

'Is your contact someone in the police?' She had noticed how he had lowered his eyes from her as he spoke, as though to curtail their flirtatious inclinations.

He nodded. 'There are others, but the man we're pinning all our hopes on is the Chief Commissioner—a thoroughly decent man by the name of Vincent Mbeye.'

'He must be taking quite a risk—planning to allow two prisoners to escape. Why would he do such a thing?'

'His immediate reason is that Fred, my cameraman, received quite a beating at the hands of the soldiers. That's something I only learned on the flight back,' he added grimly as Sophie gave a groan of horror. 'But his main reasons go much deeper than that—to the coup itself and what motivated it.' He leaned forward and poured himself more coffee. 'Vincent Mbeye is one of only a handful of Gamborrans who know the full tawdry story—though, as you're no doubt aware, the vast majority of ordinary Gamborrans are opposed to the coup on straightforward principle.'

Sophie nodded. 'You mentioned it being essential that the Spanish Embassy remain open—why?' she asked.

'It's the last remaining link with the outside world for those opposed to the coup.' He shook his head grimly. 'The whole thing would be laughable if it weren't for the possibility of it all turning very nasty.'

'What—a counter-coup?' The mere thought of the bloodshed such an event might bring filled her with horror.

'God forbid! Gamborra has never run to an army— the police are given the rudiments of military training, but they most certainly don't constitute a fighting force. It's keeping the lid on a spontaneous uprising of the people that's the problem, and managing to do so till it all blows over.'

'How do you mean—blows over?'

'It's a little complicated, but a few years back a team of UN geologists were called into Gamborra to investigate some pretty strange geological readings emanating from there. On paper, the entire central region promised to be a virtual Aladdin's cave of incalculable wealth—precious stones, minerals and metals just waiting to be plundered. It all turned out to be a bizarre geological freak ... something that has been known before in similar geographical locations. Obviously a bunch of greedy chancers has got hold of the original reports ... they're in for one hell of a rude awakening once the true facts come to light.'

'And you think they'll just pack up and leave once that happens?' asked Sophie.

He nodded.

'How soon is that likely to be?'

'Hard to say—it could be a matter of weeks, rather than months . . . it depends on how soon they set their geologists to work, and how long it takes them to face the facts with which those geologists will inevitably present them. The longer it takes, the harder the task for Mbeye and the chiefs from whom he and his colleagues are enlisting support.'

'Surely the obvious thing would be to tell the coup ringleaders the truth,' protested Sophie.

'These men aren't a cosy African equivalent of the Surrey Constabulary!' he exclaimed impatiently. 'It would be tantamount to signing his own death warrant for Mbeye and the others even to hint they had an inkling of the true reasons behind the coup. For God's sake, Sophie, the shot-gun behind our marriage was the regime's pathological secretiveness!'

'I'm sorry—I suppose it *was* a pretty stupid thing to say,' she sighed, helping herself to more coffee.

'Except that in a way you're perfectly right,' he sighed, confusing her. 'Had there been any copies of the reports scuppering the original surveys available, they might have done the trick. Unfortunately no one anywhere was able to come up with a single one.' He glanced at his watch as he finished speaking. 'I have to see a couple of people in a short while. Will you be all right here on your own?'

Sophie nodded, her mind so preoccupied with digesting what she had been told that her pulse-rate scarcely altered when he rose and gently ruffled her hair before leaving the room.

CHAPTER FOUR

'JUST who do you think you are?' raged Sophie, any traces of her earlier feelings of well-being, already decimated by the group of reporters who had converged on her like a ravening pack, now completely dispelled by the vociferous fury of the man confronting her in the hall of the flat. 'I'm not your prisoner! If I want to go out, I'll damn well go out!'

'You'll damn well do as you're told!' yelled Patrick Carlisle after her as she stormed off down the corridor and into her room. 'You've about as much idea of how to handle the Press as I have of brain surgery,' he continued, bursting into the room behind her. 'Who was that black guy you were talking to?'

'Do you mean to tell me you were watching?' exploded Sophie. 'You actually watched what was going on out there and you didn't lift a finger to stop it?'

'I told you not to go out,' he informed her with venomous satisfaction. 'I warned you they'd really lay into you if I weren't around—and you've already had a taste of what they're like with me there.'

'Yes, I have, haven't I?' she hit back maliciously. 'Your little black book, or whatever it is in which you list your conquests, must contain the names of just about every female reporter there is—and now they're all queueing up to sharpen their claws on me!'

'Spare me the histrionics,' he drawled, ramming his hands in his pockets as he leaned one shoulder against the door-frame. 'I asked you who the black guy was.'

69

'A representative from *Playboy* wanting me to do a centrefold,' she snapped, shrugging out of her coat. 'He was a reporter like the rest of them, for heaven's sake! Now, would you mind getting out, I want to get changed?'

'He wasn't a reporter,' he retorted, ignoring her request.

'He *was*! He was from the *Gamborran Echo*.'

'There's no such paper. What did he say to you?'

'He wanted to know if we'd heard from Fred and José,' she replied, now acutely aware of the sharp tension in his body, despite its overtly relaxed posture.

'And what did you tell him?' he asked, something in his tone acting like a damper on her fury.

'I . . . I can't remember exactly,' she stammered. 'Naturally I said we hadn't heard from them.'

'I'd like you to remember—to remember *exactly* what was said,' he told her, a menacing softness in his words.

'I've already told you!' she exclaimed, furious with herself for the ease with which he had thrown her on the defensive. 'I said we hadn't heard from them— that we couldn't possibly expect to hear from two people in police custody. Satisfied?' Yet she knew she had said the wrong thing in the instant the words were out—from his sharp intake of breath followed immediately by a soft strong of Spanish oaths. She had said the wrong thing, but what constituted its wrongness she had no idea. All she knew was that during the past three days of topsy-turvy confusion she had probably picked up enough swear words in this man's mother tongue to enable her to make the average Spanish sailor blush to his roots. 'That you do it in Spanish, rather than English, doesn't alter the fact that you're swearing at me. I don't like being sworn at!'

'I'm not swearing at you—I'm using a well-known psychological ploy for letting off steam. And you can consider yourself lucky I haven't my hands round your throat! I asked you not to go out alone because I didn't want you waylaid by the Press or any other interested parties.' His face was pale with anger as he straightened suddenly. 'My reasons for making such a request—and believe me, a request was all it was, despite your childish conviction that I issue you with orders—were solely to protect the interests of my crew,' he intoned with chilling softness. 'I was under the misapprehension that deep down you were actually an adult. The fact that José and Fred are in police—as opposed to military—custody is information we could only possess because it had been leaked to us.'

Sophie felt the colour drain from her face. She sank weakly on to the dressing-table stool, her head shaking slowly from side to side as though the action might create a miracle and erase the information she had so carelessly—so stupidly—imparted.

'Oh, God, it just didn't occur to me,' she whispered, stunned. 'I should have thought...Patrick, I'm so sorry.'

'There are people in Gamborra taking immense risks on behalf of friends of mine—people whose lives could be in jeopardy because someone such as you didn't trouble to think.' His eyes fixed on hers, cold and implacable. 'Loyalty is one area where you'll find I'm Spaniard through and through. I *owe* these people for the risks they are taking, and I'll owe them till my dying day. And I'll do everything in my power to give them whatever protection I can for as long as they need it.'

'I've already said how sorry I am!' she exclaimed defensively. 'I know nothing can excuse my unforgivable thoughtlessness, but it would never have happened if you'd taken the trouble to sit down and explain things to me. When you *are* here—which hasn't been all that often—you're either treating everything I say as some sort of pathetic joke, or you're ranting at me for one ludicrous reason or another. I loathe this unnatural situation every bit as much as you do, but you've no right whatsoever to assume I'm incapable of worrying about your friends just because I don't know them! I want their safe return as much as you do. But you don't exactly make it easy for me to help in any way... all it would have taken would have been a few words of warning——' She broke off, struggling for composure. 'And whatever you say about making requests, you *do* make it sound as though you're issuing orders... a habit my father has to perfection and which he too always regards as no more than perfectly reasonable requests.'

'Perhaps he does—I wouldn't know,' he muttered dismissively. 'But then I don't happen to be your father.'

She rose, drained by the anger and guilt seething with equal intensity within her. 'Patrick, who was that man?'

'I honestly don't know,' he replied quietly, turning. 'I'm probably letting my imagination run away with me. For all I know he's no more than a tenacious freelancer hoping for another angle to the story.' He gave a small, oddly weary shrug. 'You get changed and I'll put the kettle on.'

She followed him into the corridor. 'But that's not what you think—you think he's some sort of agent for the regime.'

'Even if he were—and the more I think about it, the more fanciful it seems—you wouldn't necessarily have done any harm.'

'For heaven's sake, Patrick!' she exclaimed, following him into the kitchen. 'You may find this hard to believe, but I prefer your ranting to your heavy-handed attempts at kindness. Of course I've done harm if the man's an agent!'

'You know, you're an impossible woman to please, Carlisle,' he muttered exasperatedly. 'I'd no intention of trying to be kind—I'm the ogre who rants and issues orders, remember? It merely occurred to me that—assuming the man actually was a spy or whatever—he probably wouldn't have read any particular significance into your remark. After all, when someone is arrested, it's usually by the police.'

'But they know I was there—that I'd be aware of the difference between the police and the militia,' she parried suspiciously.

'Ah, but you're a mere woman.' He grinned, picking up the kettle and filling it. 'Even you must have noticed the average male Gamborran's attitude to women. They'd probably consider technical subtleties, such as the differing roles of the police and the militia, beyond you.'

'You *are* being kind!' she exclaimed accusingly, watching as he put far too much tea into the pot—he made particularly lousy tea, she mused inconsequentially, even worse than his coffee.

'OK, have it your way—I'm kindness personified. Did you get more lemons?'

She handed him a lemon from a full bowl practically under his nose and watched as he cut it into wedges. 'Patrick, whoever that man was... I've learned a lesson.' And perhaps he had learned one too—the danger of keeping her so completely in the dark—though she doubted it.

'And what's that?' he asked conversationally, his eyes still on his task. 'To be a good girl and do as Patrick tells you in future?'

Flashing him a look of pure fury, she grabbed the kettle and filled it. 'I'll make my own tea, thank you, I prefer it when the spoon doesn't stand up in it,' she informed him pettily, plugging it in and switching it on and feeling unspeakably childish.

'Feel free.' He grinned, obviously quite unperturbed by her outburst. 'I meant to ask you,' he added, catching her by the shoulders then proceeding to scrutinise her thoroughly. 'What were you up to when you were on the run, Carlisle? You look kind of different.'

'I got new glasses,' she mumbled, refusing to meet his gaze. 'The others were driving me mad.'

'Yes, that's what it must be,' he murmured, nodding his head sagely as he continued his inspection.

Sophie's eyes flew to his in outraged disbelief. She had also had her mutilated hair properly styled, her eyelashes tinted because of the problems she was still having using mascara, and a toning facial. She had had all that done because she was sick and tired of looking so depressingly drab... and now he was quite happy to attribute what she knew had to be her vastly improved appearance to a pair of trendy sunglasses!

'It's amazing what a difference changing your glasses can make,' he continued, the look in his eyes in total conflict with his lightness of tone. 'Now I can actually see how perfect an oval your face is; how delicately boned and straight your nose is, apart from its sassy little tip. And as for your mouth——'

'Very droll,' she interrupted, the crushing sarcasm she had intended marred by the husky breathlessness unfortunately distorting her tone.

'To be truthful, I can't really say the new glasses do anything for your mouth,' he mused, showing no signs of allowing himself to by side-tracked as he painstakingly traced the outline of her lips with his forefinger—a gesture that brought a silent groan of resignation from her as her pulses immediately began running amok. 'It still turns up at the corners, and it's still the sexiest little organ of communication it's ever been my privilege to sample.' His head, which had begun lowering towards hers as he uttered those husky, slightly uneven words, jerked to a sudden halt as hers tilted back, her lips parted in anticipation of his. 'My tea should be more than brewed by now,' he announced matter-of-factly, releasing her and stepping away. 'And you still haven't got around to making yours.'

Feeling exactly as she imagined she might had someone left her dangling over the edge of a precipice supported by nothing more than a single thread, Sophie tried desperately to bring a small degree of order to the mental and emotional chaos now buffeting her. He wasn't normal, she comforted herself as her dazed eyes followed his every movement. There was a lithe grace in his tall, lean body as he reached up for the cups, and a fascinating combination of strength and elegance in the hands that deftly grasped them ... but the man just was not normal. She knew what she had seen in his eyes—in their smoky green darkness in that moment before he had so abruptly brought down the shutters... or did she? Perhaps she was the abnormal one... merely imagining she was seeing in his eyes a mirror image of the turbulent intensity of her own confusing feelings.

'I've poured you some of this, but you'd best water it down to your own taste.' he announced, dropping a wedge of lemon into his own cup. 'Let's go into the living-room and you can tell me what else you've done with your day—apart from buying new glasses.' He picked up the cup and walked to the door. 'Are you coming?'

'Yes,' she muttered, thrown to find how noticeably her hands were shaking as she added water to the sludge-coloured tea. This was ridiculous, she remonstrated with herself; she was allowing this abnormal situation to get to her to the extent that she was incapable of rational thought. She was becoming obsessed—there was hardly a moment in her waking day not filled with mulling over one facet or another of him, and most of the time she couldn't even decide whether she liked or loathed him.

With an exclamation of impatience with herself, she picked up her cup and and followed him into the living-room.

He was sitting on one of the armchairs, his feet propped on the coffee-table and crossed at the ankles. He glanced across at her, relaxed and smiling, as she placed her drink on the table and sat down on the sofa.

'I've been thinking how little I know about you,' he stated. 'Perhaps you should tell me something about yourself—at least that's a safe subject.'

'How do you mean—safe?' she asked, puzzled.

'Well, decidedly *not* safe was that clinch we almost ended up in just now in the kitchen,' he stated mildly, picking up his cup.

Sophie said nothing, but she had no control over the small smile that crept across her lips, nor the warm feeling that was oddly akin to relief now spreading through her.

'Superhuman though I'm finding my powers of self-restraint to be, I doubt if even they could have stood another bout of your looking at me as though I'd mortally wounded you.'

'I didn't mean to,' she blurted out. 'It's just——' She made a quick dive for her cup to silence herself.

'It's just what?' He grinned. 'One thing I can't stand is someone starting to say something then clamming up.'

His teasing, quizzical eyes remained steadfastly on hers as she drained her cup, then returned it with painstaking care to its saucer.

'Well?'

'Well . . . it's just that I thought you hadn't felt anything and I hated the thought of having all those weird feelings on my own,' she gabbled. 'It was bad enough with you feeling them too, but if you didn't . . .' Her hands rose to press her burning cheeks as her rushed spate of words petered to a stricken halt.

'Sophie, how many times do I have to tell you there's nothing weird about a bit of good old-fashioned lust?' he demanded softly. 'I can't think why people feel so obliged to give it fancy names instead of accepting it for what it is—it's a perfectly natural human feeling. What *is* weird is our circumstances, but, despite my constant balking, if it weren't for them we'd probably——' He grinned as he broke off. 'Don't waste your breath pointing out I've not finished something I started saying. I'll just give you fair warning, though, that it's gloves off between us, as far as I'm concerned, once this wretched marriage has been annulled.'

'Is that so?' she murmured huskily, while the drunken elation of her senses informed her of just how welcome his words were.

'That is very much so,' he replied with a groaned chuckle. 'But the damned thing hasn't been annulled yet, so, before we're tempted to forget that very pertinent fact, back to that safe subject I suggested... You know, I don't even know your age.'

'I'm twenty-three. How old are you?'

'Thirty-one...why are you taking off your glasses?'

'I can handle the light in here,' she protested, as he immediately switched off the lamp nearest him.

'I'm not sure I can, though,' he drawled, his eyes flicking over her. 'Your hair's different.' His tone was almost accusing.

'I had the hacked bits evened out by a hairdresser—I used to have it quite long, but the sisters had to cut it,' she muttered, feeling suddenly gauche and ill at ease.

'It suits you like that...pixie-ish...very sexy. Why don't you get on with your father?'

Though his abrupt change of subject threw her slightly, Sophie was only too happy to follow its direction away from the highly charged, slightly menacing atmosphere that seemed to hover in the air between them.

'It's not that I don't get on with him,' she sighed. 'It's just that when I'd told him I'd decided to take up nursing, I might as well have announced I was going on the streets, the way he reacted.'

'But he's in medicine himself.' Patrick frowned.

'Yes, and he's very popular with his nurses. He was one of the first consultants to give them active support over pay and conditions ... it's a profession he holds in the highest regard.'

'So?' he prompted as she fell silent, lost in her own private thoughts.

'It's just that he's autocratic, to put it mildly, and he'd decided his daughter was going to become a doctor—my mother's one too, she's in renal research—in fact, I'd already got a place in medical school...'

'And?' he prompted again, as again she lapsed into silence.

She gave a small shrug. 'I think I grew up ... out of the blue. I woke up one morning—it was very early, well before dawn —and I couldn't get back to sleep. And suddenly I found myself thinking—I mean *really* thinking—in a way I hadn't done before. Odd memories kept leaping into my mind ... such as the way my father had begun nagging me at quite an early age about chemistry and biology being my weakest subjects, and how I'd need good results in both for medical school. You can't imagine the hours and hours of extra coaching he insisted on.'

'Did it have the desired effect?' he asked, a hint of amusement in his tone.

'It worked,' she snapped, uncomfortable with her memories. 'Anyway, as I was thinking I began to see that somewhere along the line my father had managed to drum his wishes into me—to the extent that I accepted I would eventually become a doctor much in the same way as I accepted that I would one day become an adult... Does that make any sense to you?'

He nodded, motioning her to continue as he removed his feet from the table and let them sprawl untidily beneath it.

'That morning, it was as though I'd been able to step out of myself and see myself as an uninvolved spectator. It was easy then to see that I'd never really made any choice—my father had decided and I'd just gone along with his decision, somehow believing it had been mine.'

'It can't be said you carried your rebellion to extremes—you didn't opt out of medicine completely.'

'You don't understand,' she sighed. 'I wasn't rebelling against him. All I did was have a good think about things and realise I was far more suited to becoming a nurse than a doctor.'

'So what was your mother's reaction to all this?' he asked.

'She was completely on my side.' She hesitated. 'It's a bit difficult to explain—you see, my mother just about lives and breathes her research... and before you jump to any conclusions to the contrary, I had a very happy childhood and never once felt in the least neglected,' she added defensively. 'My mother, as you probably saw, is very gentle and rather vague at times, whereas Daddy's very quick-tempered and—much like you—manages to get his own way more often than not.'

He flashed her a look of pained indignation which quickly deteriorated into a broad grin.

'Anyway, I told my father I'd decided to do nursing—fully expecting his complete support—and suddenly all hell was let loose. My mother, who was also completely thrown by his reaction, suggested I ignore what she termed his little tantrum and promptly took off to do a six-month research stint in Canada.'

'And father's little tantrum?'

'It was more a question of full-scale war for several weeks—but by then I'd moved into the nurses' hostel and started my training.'

'And the war continued?'

'On and off,' she sighed, bristling at the memory of how stubbornly her father had refused to accept facts, taking every opportunity to blame any ill that befell her on her decision to go against his wishes. 'I suppose you could say we managed to rub along fairly gingerly whenever I was at home ... then Steven got married and it all erupted again.'

'Who's Steven?' he exclaimed. 'I somehow got the impression you were an only child.'

'I am. Steven ... I suppose he could be described as the traditional boy next door. He'd been my boyfriend since I was seventeen ... we were sort of engaged.'

'You don't say! And the devil upped and married another,' he teased in an exaggerated Irish brogue.

'Do you want to hear this or not?' she demanded.

'Poor Sophie,' he murmured contritely. 'I'd no right to be flippant. Were you very upset?'

'I was livid,' she chuckled. 'Steven and I had become stuck in a ridiculous rut. There weren't that many people our age around where we lived ... I doubt if we were ever really in love. But I'd agreed to become unofficially engaged to him when I started my course.

What really infuriated me when he suddenly got married was all those new and exciting and most tempting men whose attentions I'd been virtuously spurning on his account!'

'So where does Papa feature in all this?' he asked.

'The truth is, my father's the most dreadful snob. Because Steven stood to inherit some minor title or other from a bachelor uncle, Daddy couldn't wait to welcome him as a son-in-law. And according to him, Steven had been shattered by my lack of guts and determination in discarding my true vocation—I'm quoting Daddy here, by the way, and should point out that Steven had given me every encouragement— and that his faith in me had been brutally destroyed——' She broke off as he made a sudden convulsive movement. 'I'm glad you find my traumatic life story so very amusing,' she informed him, having difficulty keeping her own face straight as she watched his vain attempts to do the same.

'This is far better than anything I've ever read,' he choked. 'Do carry on.'

'I trust I'm going to find your life history equally entertaining when the time comes,' she retorted, grinning broadly. 'Anyway, I've forgotten where I was!'

'Papa was ranting about your having driven Steven from the fold,' he supplied obligingly.

Sophie gave a soft chuckle of exasperation. 'You have a decidedly suspect sense of humour, Patrick Carlisle,' she admonished, then continued. 'My father eventually simmered down again and then . . . I'm not sure I should be telling you this,' she teased primly. 'Oh, all right, then,' she added hastily as he picked up a cushion and took threatening aim with it. 'With

Steven no longer around to remain faithful to, I'd begun investigating some of those interesting men I mentioned. Not an easy task when I'd spent the best part of a year holding them at bay so virtuously. Anyway, along came Robert...'

As the muted burr of the telephone brought her words to a trailed halt, he leapt to his feet with an exclamation of impatience and went to answer it.

And while he spoke into the mouthpiece, Sophie found herself scrutinising him, her fascinated gaze caught up in the supple movements of his lips as they formed and uttered words to which her ears had become deaf, so great was her concentration on simply watching. Then her gaze faltered as she was remembering the tingling anticipation on her own lips as they had vainly awaited the explosive excitement of his.

She liked him all right, she told herself with a small stab of alarm. He was fascinating, provoking, infuriating... yet in his company she felt more vibrantly alive, more stimulated than she had felt with any other man she had ever known...

'That was Ed Jordan,' he announced, flinging down the receiver. 'It looks as though things might be on the move.' He moved towards the door as he spoke. 'I'll probably camp round at Ed's place tonight just to be around if Vincent Mbeye manages to get through with any news.'

'I'll be keeping my fingers crossed,' she called out, an odd sensation that was almost like loneliness gripping her in the instant she heard the door slam behind him.

She would be keeping her fingers crossed for the event that would put an end to all this, she told herself warily, conscious that she was suppressing positive feelings of disappointment. Then she leaned back against the sofa, a soft, dreamy smile curving her lips. He had admitted it was the weirdness of their circumstances against which he constantly balked.

'It's gloves off between us, as far as I'm concerned, once this wretched marriage has been annulled.'

The remembered words drifted through her, filling her with the softness of promise, fuelling a growing impatience within her to discover what it was that might lie ahead.

CHAPTER FIVE

IT WAS shortly after dawn that Sophie heard Patrick's key in the lock and the sound of the door closing behind him. Leaping from her bed and flinging on a robe, she raced out into the hall.

'Any news?' she asked excitedly.

He finished removing his overcoat then turned, his expression curiously blank as he regarded her—almost as though he had momentarily forgotten her existence.

'Patrick, what's happened?' she asked, her excitement doused by a sudden surge of anxiety.

'Go back to bed,' he muttered wearily, walking past her and into the kitchen.

'I couldn't possibly sleep,' she protested, following him and switching on the light. 'Has something gone wrong?' she asked quietly, trying desperately not to wince as the sudden brightness burned savagely against her eyes.

'Things certainly haven't gone right,' he muttered, his face gaunt beneath the dark stubble of beard and completely without expression as he filled the percolator and began ladling coffee into its filter. 'Right now, I need to unwind—so would you mind if I explained later?'

'Of course not,' she replied at once, moving to his side. 'Let me do that.' She took the coffee canister from his unresisting grasp. He looked ghastly. 'You go and lie down—you look whacked...in fact, are you sure coffee's such a good idea? It'll keep you awake.'

'I need to be kept awake,' he muttered, his hands producing a rasping sound as he rubbed them wearily against his stubbled face. 'I'll have a shower while that's perking,' he added, reaching out and ruffling her hair in a gesture that was detached—almost absent-minded. 'I didn't mean to disturb you. Go back to bed and try to get some sleep.'

She was frowning as she watched his retreating figure—he was almost stumbling from exhaustion. Then she finished preparing the coffee and went to the fridge. She had no idea when he had last eaten— certainly nothing before going out last night, she re- alised with a pang of worry. Then she gave a soft groan of disbelief. She was fussing over him exactly like one of those women she couldn't abide...if he was hungry, he was perfectly capable of doing something about it himself! She was on the verge of hurling shut the fridge door when she hesitated. On the other hand, he *had* been up all night, probably sick with worry over two people who meant a very great deal to him...and whatever news he had had, it certainly wasn't good.

By the time he emerged from the shower—damp- haired and shaved and wrapped in a snowy white tow- elling robe that accentuated the rich Mediterranean gold of his skin—Sophie's feelings, about the two egg and bacon sandwiches she brought in to him in the living-room along with the coffee, had swung full circle.

'I thought I told you to go back to bed,' he mut- tered ungraciously, his glance cursory as she placed the tray on the table and handed him the plate and a napkin.

'And I told you I couldn't possibly sleep,' she retorted sharply—he could at least have thanked her for the trouble she had gone to! 'Just because I've never met them, it doesn't mean I'm incapable of worrying about your friends,' she added quietly, prompted by a sudden stab of guilt. 'After all you've done for me, I...I feel somehow a part of all this...I...' She halted her stammered words with a shrug of embarrassment, uncertain exactly what it was she had been trying to say.

'Sophie, I'm sorry,' he sighed, patting the sofa beside him and smiling wanly at her. 'Come and sit down and have your breakfast and I'll try explaining.'

She sat down. 'They're both for you,' she muttered diffidently, leaning forward and pouring two cups of coffee. 'I'm not hungry.'

'Come on—just half a one,' he coaxed. 'Delicious though I'm sure they are, I can't possibly manage two.'

In the end she accepted half a sandwich, acutely conscious of the coiled tension in him as he ate, despite the air of relaxed intimacy between them.

'Mbeye got through to us a couple of hours ago,' he told her. 'The original plan was for the police to move Fred and José north, close to the Zaire border. It seems things were going beautifully to plan until a military unit intercepted them on the way north—claiming both men were needed for further questioning.'

'Oh, no,' groaned Sophie, a sick fear gripping her.

'Contrary to the orders they'd been given, the police escort refused to comply. And as I've already explained, the last thing they want is open confrontation between the police and the regime. Before they know where they are they could have a full-scale uprising on their hands.'

'Why on earth did the police disobey their orders?' asked Sophie, her fears deepening as she saw the harsh set to his mouth as he helped himself to more coffee.

'I told you Fred had been beaten,' he stated grimly. 'So badly, it seems, that the escort balked at handing him back for what they felt certain would be more of the same. They managed to stall—demanding written authority for the hand-over—and while all the arguing was going on, they let them slip away.'

'So they're free!' exclaimed Sophie.

'They're on the run with God knows how many troops out hunting them,' he corrected tonelessly. 'The regime are probably now convinced they definitely *had* something to hide... and what's more, they know damn well the police instigated their escape, no matter how much it's denied. Mbeye was taking a risk even making an overseas call. We know how paranoid they are about secrecy, but not the degree of their sophistication—not that it takes too much of that to tap phones, even on a pretty wide scale.'

'So what do you think Fred's and José's chances are of making it to the border?' she asked quietly. 'I'm sure they could rely on every assistance possible from local Gamborrans.'

'Mbeye's hoping they'll head south-east—to the Zambian border,' he replied pensively. 'It's a long trek, but the regime will be concentrating their search along the border with Zaire. Of course, Mbeye's right... except that José's bound to stick out like a sore thumb.'

Sophie glanced at him puzzlement.

'Fred's black,' he explained. 'He also has an almost phenomenal command of east and central African dialects—languages are something of a hobby with him and he's nothing short of brilliant at them.' His face softened into a reminiscent smile. 'It took Fred a matter of months to become pretty well fluent in Spanish, after which José's English—never exactly intelligible to start with—deteriorated at a rate of knots.'

'How long have the three of you worked together?' asked Sophie.

'About seven years. We met, believe it or not, in an Algerian gaol,' he added with a grin. 'Fred was doing sound with one of the big American networks, José was with RTVE—Spanish television, and I was freelancing for the BBC.'

'How on earth did you all land up in gaol?'

'We got caught up in a demonstration that deteriorated into a full-scale riot—as it turned out, prison was about the safest place we could have ended up in at that particular time.'

'You've certainly led exciting lives, one way or another,' she remarked with a hint of wistfulness. 'And it seems to me that Fred and José would be far better equipped than most to get themselves out of somewhere like Gamborra.'

He turned and looked at her, a slow smile creeping across his face. 'Strangely enough, I think I needed reminding of that. I'm so close to all this, I'm not seeing it clearly, but you're right—those two are past masters at getting themselves out of tight spots.'

'So—how about you trying to get some sleep?' suggested Sophie briskly, rising and stacking the tray. 'You must be exhausted.'

'I've told you—I shan't be sleeping,' he answered, the brusqueness of his tone to some extent negated by the fact that he was still smiling. 'But if you insist on mothering me, how about another pot of coffee?'

'I had no intention of mothering you,' she snapped, lifting the tray as she felt the colour rush to her cheeks. 'You'd been up all night and I made you a couple of sandwiches—I'd have done the same for a stray dog!'

'What—egg and bacon sandwiches?' he murmured with wide-eyed innocence, as she marched to the door.

'More than likely,' she retorted. 'Anyway, I'm off to bed—I need some sleep, even if you don't.'

She deposited the tray in the kitchen, the initial determination in her stride waning as she reached her room. Why on earth had she flown off the handle like that? Her reaction had been out of all proportion to his harmlessly teasing words, she fumed with herself. And it was hardly his fault she had had that ridiculous battle with herself as to whether or not she should have made those damned sandwiches in the first place! And flouncing out like that had been petty in the extreme. No matter how he might appear on the surface, deep down he was obviously desperately worried and, instead of reacting with the compassion that would hitherto have come normally to her, she was pandering to prima donna tendencies she had never dreamed she possessed. Torn between guilt and confusion, she eyed her bed balefully. Sleep was certainly out of the question, just as was returning and facing him with rationality and understanding— something all that was decent in her told her she should now be doing.

After several moments' frowning hesitation, she decided she would first have a bath, an act of procrastination admittedly, but one caused more by common sense than by cowardice, she consoled herself, because she most certainly needed a little time in which to collect her thoughts... There was so much she owed him, the least of which was collecting her wits about her to offer him what support he might need for the moment.

As she finished towelling herself dry and began dressing, it was the knowledge of how completely uncharacteristically she had been behaving that filled her mind—niggling away at her with the unpleasant persistence of an aching tooth. If she were completely honest with herself, she would be forced to admit that her entire pattern of behaviour, since Patrick had burst into her life, had been more or less consistently out of character, she told herself with a sigh, then went to the mirror and began examining herself critically. Thank heavens she still had a tan, she mused, a small frown creasing her brow—her face looked almost drawn. Her frown deepened as her critical eyes rose to the cropped gleam of auburn hugging her head like a shining cap. It was this wretched hairstyle making her look drawn, she told herself, giving an exclamation of exasperation as she impatiently ruffled her fingers through her hair. It made her look childish—almost like a boy! Glowering at her gamine reflection, she tried to visualise her hair as it had been—thick and luxuriant and tumbling to her shoulders. Robert had loved running his fingers through it, something she had loved him doing until that ghastly day she had discovered he had a wife back home in Australia.

She gave a small shudder as she turned away from the mirror. At least the memory no longer hurt. And at least her heart had not had time to become involved to the extent that it had been badly damaged. Though Robert had claimed to have an 'open' marriage—whatever that was supposed to mean—when she had angrily confronted him, nothing could alter the fact it was a marriage he had gone to great pains to conceal from her, she remembered with disgust. And now, less than a year later, she could scarcely recall his features in detail, she realised in pleased amazement. She closed her eyes, trying to conjure up that face she had once come close to loving, a rueful, chuckling groan escaping her as Patrick's outrageously handsome features leapt with distracting clarity into her mind. For all his undoubted faults, treachery in marriage, she was certain, would never be one of them—his decidedly edgy attitude to their own bogus marriage told her that. And it was just as well he had such strong feelings on the subject, she told herself as a jumpy, uneasy feeling settled on her...with Patrick there could be none of the holding back she had—mercifully—found relatively easy with Robert. And with Patrick her heart would be open to damage beyond repair if ever it made the mistake of becoming involved. She stood motionless in the centre of the room as thought after disconcerting thought began crowding into her mind, becoming so lost in them that the soft rap on the door that broke through them made her start visibly.

'Come in,' she called—words that were purely reflex.

'Thank God you're running true to form!' exclaimed Patrick as he stepped into the room.

'I beg your pardon?' muttered Sophie, her thoughts scattering.

'I told you to go to bed, so the odds were you'd be up,' he explained humourlessly. 'Pack your bags—we're going to Madrid.'

Sophie was still trying to work out which of several things she had found the most galling during the past hours as they stepped into a taxi in the comparatively balmy air of a late Madrid afternoon. There was the fact that she had lost the blazing and protracted exchange that had developed from his initial abrupt command for her to pack—and command was its only just description. Then there was the humiliating fact that on several occasions during these past interminable hours her plagued eyes had necessitated her burying her face against the shelter of his body in order to escape the agonising glare of light. And then there was . . .

'How long do you intend maintaining this martyred silence, Carlisle?' he snapped unsympathetically. 'I hope you realise that, unless you plan taking a crash course in Spanish, I'm likely to be the only person with whom you're able to communicate.'

'Your father speaks English, doesn't he?' she retorted huffily. To think that for one foolish moment she had actually worried that she might be getting emotionally involved with this . . . this supercilious, dictatorial creature!

'So does my mother—albeit with a delightfully Irish accent.'

Sophie flashed him a look that was intended to wither while also conveying triumph.

'Perhaps I forgot to mention that my parents are leaving for Ireland this evening,' he added with casual unconcern.

For what was no more than a fraction of a second, Sophie contemplated counting in an attempt to control her anger and decided, in virtually the same instant, to save herself the bother.

'This gift you have of rendering others speechless with rage and confusion,' she managed through viciously clamped teeth, 'is it something you were blessed with from birth, or did it take some years to perfect?'

'Rendering you speechless—and the past few hours of your self-imposed silence doesn't count—is something I have yet to master,' he murmured blandly. 'So whatever it is you've been bottling up during that time, I dare say you're about to let rip with now——' He broke off with a grin that struck her as particularly evil—an interpretation that was immediately vindicated when he suddenly made a grab for her, placing one arm round her shoulder and the hand of the other firmly across her mouth. 'Stop struggling and listen,' he ordered in a whisper. 'Whatever you have to say, you can do so without resorting to screeching at me like a fishwife as you did back in London. I don't fancy the idea of the driver's ordering us out of his cab for brawling—so nod if you agree not to yell.'

The look she gave him would have shrivelled even an only moderately sensitive person—his responding laughter served to confirm her every suspicion as to his total lack of sensitivity.

'OK—we spend the next half-hour or so with you gagged,' he informed her easily.

After several fruitless seconds of intensely eloquent glaring, Sophie accepted she had no option but to capitulate. She nodded.

'Have I your word?'

Again she nodded, consoling herself with the fact that, had her teeth been able to gain any purchase whatever on his hand, she would have had no qualms about biting it right through to the bone.

'Right, fire away—but quietly,' he said, removing his hand but not his arm.

Though shaking with fury, Sophie managed to keep her words down to a venomous whisper as she hurled them at him. 'You're enough to reduce a saint to screeching at you like a fishwife,' she hissed. 'You told me to feel free to remind you of the publicity you were getting from this damned marriage—so I'm reminding you! There was absolutely no need for you to remind me of my indebtedness to you to get me to agree to coming here!'

'You could have fooled me,' he retorted. 'You were already practically foaming at the mouth by the time I felt it necessary to stoop to that tactic.'

'There would be no need to stoop to *any* tactics with me if you'd only stop ordering me about!' she exclaimed in exasperation.

'Your trouble is you're too sensitive—or perhaps I mean paranoid.'

'If your definition of paranoia is objecting to being ordered to pack my bags and take off at an instant's notice, then yes, I'm quite definitely paranoid,' she retaliated frigidly.

'OK, I worded it rather abruptly,' he conceded, with no discernible trace of apology. 'I happened to have other things on my mind at the time.'

'Yes!' hissed Sophie. 'Your parents' reaction to the marriage! You led me to believe it was necessary to hotfoot it over here to pacify them—now you tell me they're on their way to Ireland!'

He gave her a look she found impossible to interpret as he suddenly removed his arm from around her.

'I led you to believe no such thing,' he informed her coldly. 'If you remember, you were so busy ranting that it was virtually impossible for you to hear anything I attempted to say.'

'I suggest you try telling me again—now,' she retorted, finding it impossible to ignore the small voice inside her pointing out that she probably wouldn't have heard the roof caving in over them, so total had been her earlier fury—a fury that had been completely justified, as far as she was concerned.

'I've forgotten—that was all hours ago,' he informed her in tones of weary boredom.

Suppressing a strong urge to resort to shrieking at him, she took a deep breath. 'Don't be ridiculous. You can't possibly have forgotten the reasons for our having to drop everything and hare over here.'

'Let's just say I felt like a change of scenery,' he drawled uncooperatively. 'It will also be a relief to escape the attentions of the British Press—we Spaniards don't go in for that sort of carry-on.'

This time it was not so much verbal as physical abuse Sophie was restraining herself from hurling at him. With his infuriatingly pious tones he had not only managed to lump her along with the British Press, but had actually seemed to imply he held her personally responsible for their actions by dint of her shared nationality with them.

'You're as near as damn it part of that same horde yourself,' she reminded him, her words coming out in a frustrated squeak.

'So I am,' he accepted without rancour, turning and giving her a smile of such innocent sweetness that she found herself almost drowning in the huge wave of suspicion washing over her. 'You'd better compose yourself—we've arrived.'

'I'm perfectly composed,' she lied, unaccountably feeling almost sick with nervousness and apprehension.

'That's good to hear,' he murmured, as the taxi drove through an arched entrance and into a courtyard. 'Perhaps you'll be able to give me a bit of moral support—you see, what with one thing and another, I never actually got round to telling my parents about the marriage.' He grinned as he reached over and placed his forefinger under her chin. 'Stop gawping, Carlisle, it really doesn't become you.'

CHAPTER SIX

SOPHIE watched as the tall, similarly built figures of Patrick and his father weaved their way around the mound of dust-sheeted furniture dominating the high-ceilinged drawing-room, then disappeared through huge double doors. She turned slightly, her heart in her mouth as her gaze met the cool green of a pair of disconcertingly familiar eyes. Maria Carlisle was one of the most exquisitely beautiful women Sophie had ever seen, but there was a decided wariness in her eyes whenever they alighted on the stranger Patrick had brought home with him—a marked contrast to the unmistakable warmth illuminating them whenever they were on her son or husband.

'Perhaps it would be an idea if I were to show you the kitchen,' she remarked, her words cutting across Sophie's uncomfortable thoughts. 'It's about the only relatively inhabitable room in the entire apartment at the moment,' she added, as Sophie began following her slim, dauntingly elegant figure through the doorway and out into the hall. 'Apart from Patrick's, that is.'

Any mother would have been thrown—to say the least—to hear news as odd as Patrick's, rationalised Sophie as they entered a large, farm-style kitchen. And Maria Carlisle had taken it with remarkable calm. Though calm was hardly the word to describe Michael Carlisle's reaction, she thought, amusement penetrating her gloom—initially it had been one of mild disbelief, followed quickly by chuckling mirth. It was plainly from his father that Patrick had inherited his disconcertingly casual attitude to life.

'There's not much food in—only what I thought the decorators might need,' Maria Carlisle was saying, her eyes—uncanny replicas of those of her son—watching Sophie with that same discomfiting coolness.

'Please...you shouldn't be worrying about such things...I know my arrival must have disrupted you dreadfully as it is,' stammered Sophie, wishing the ground would open up and swallow her. 'The news of the marriage must have come as the most ghastly shock to you,' she blurted out. 'But it really won't count as a marriage once it's been annulled...and I can't begin to tell you how much I owe Patrick for what he did for me. It was the most selfless gesture anyone could possibly—— ' She broke off, conscious of the breathless jumble of her words. 'I'm sorry...I'm babbling. I——'

'Sophie, sit down...please,' said Maria Carlisle, her expression softening as she drew two chairs from under the large, scrubbed-wood table in the centre of the kitchen and sat down on one. 'Do you mind if I call you Sophie—or would you prefer Mrs Carlisle?' she added, a definite twinkle softening her eyes as she invitingly patted the chair beside hers.

'I'd probably find myself turning round to see who you were addressing if you did,' replied Sophie, the tentative beginnings of a smile relaxing her tense features as she sat down. 'I'm still having great difficulty believing all this has happened—so heaven knows how you must be feeling.'

'Pretty much as you do—but it's not as though it's the end of the world,' murmured the older woman, all trace of coldness gone from her gaze as she gave Sophie's shoulder a light, reassuring pat. 'But I should like to hear the story from you,' she added. 'I found it a little puzzling that our son should choose to explain to us exclusively in Spanish—a language of which I understand you have no knowledge.'

Sophie's eyes widened in momentary bemusement. When Patrick, after having made introductions in English, had so pointedly switched to Spanish, she had been disconcerted to find herself feeling hurt and somehow excluded. Then she had retreated into a shell, deciding she was probably overreacting as usual. Now his mother seemed also to have had reservations about it.

'I'm sure Patrick's told you everything—there's really not that much to tell,' she stated diffidently. But there was, she discovered as, time and again, Maria Carlisle steered her away from the bare bones of her story and probed—with obvious and sympathetic interest—for far more personal background detail than Sophie might otherwise have given. And as she spoke, she found her earlier tension easing immeasurably. There was a fundamental warmth in Maria Carlisle that made talking to her inordinately easy.

'You poor dear! Your eyes—how do they feel now?' she exclaimed anxiously.

'Bright lights are my only real problem now—but that's only a temporary thing,' said Sophie. She hesitated, a sudden shyness in her smile. 'Mrs Carlisle, I'm sure that if Patrick hadn't had so much on his mind, he'd have contacted you and Mr Carlisle to explain about the marriage.'

Puzzlement flickered for an instant across the Spanish woman's flawless features. 'As far as Patrick knew, his father and I were on a dig in the back of beyond—Michael is an archaeologist.'

'Oh, I see,' muttered Sophie. She didn't. Once again Patrick had made not the slightest attempt to explain the facts to her.

'Unfortunately there was unseasonal rain in the site area—floods, in fact—so we were forced to return to Europe yesterday.' She pulled a small face. 'We'd arranged to have the apartment redecorated in our absence. As you can see, the decorators are ready to make a start—that's why we're off to Ireland. I'm afraid you're going to find yourself living in rather a mess, to put it very mildly.'

'I'm sure Patrick won't stay here, given these circumstances,' sighed Sophie, wondering why on earth the subject hadn't arisen when he had spoken to his parents on the phone. 'I suppose he's explained to you and your husband that his only real objection to being in London was being accosted by the Press— though their interest has more or less dwindled down to the odd die-hard, just as he said it would.' Even as she spoke, Sophie became aware that her words were having an unusual effect on the woman beside her. It was an effect she could not quite define: a slight tensing in the woman, accompanied by the merest hint of bemusement.

'Well—I'm sure things will sort themselves out,' murmured Maria Carlisle, her tone light and curiously hesitant. She gave a small start as a doorbell chimed in the distance. 'Heavens, that must be our lift to the airport.' She rose. 'I'd better find Michael,' she added apologetically, leaving a somewhat bemused Sophie still seated at the kitchen table. That feeling of kinship with Alice that she had experienced in Gamborra was back with her with a vengeance, she thought dejectedly. What was it she had said that had puzzled Patrick's mother... or was it merely her imagination working overtime?

She gave a small shake of her head in a vain attempt to clear it, then got to her feet. One of these days, thank God, all this would be behind her. For the moment, the only positive thing she could think of was to offer the Carlisles a hand with their luggage.

She made her way into the large hall and into full view of Patrick enthusiastically embracing the woman whose arms were wrapped round his neck and whose hands seemed so extraordinarily pale in contrast to the darkness of the hair against which they caressed.

Stifling feelings of almost overwhelming shock and of having intruded, she quickly retraced her steps into the kitchen. Leaning heavily against the table, she began a frantic examination of her reaction to what she had just witnessed. Of course she was shocked, she reasoned indignantly—Patrick had never even thought to warn her there was a woman in his life. And she had no way of knowing whether he had yet put the woman in the picture regarding his unforeseen marriage... had he not, she could so easily have complicated matters by bursting in on them. She had behaved with the utmost tact, she informed herself self-righteously, given that he could hardly have chosen a less private place in which to become involved in a passionate clinch.

And it was no more than tact keeping her firmly here in the kitchen, she told herself, ruthlessly crushing the one or two tentatively dissenting thoughts at-

tempting to gain hold in her mind. The only trouble
was, she admitted with a sudden pang, it would hardly
be polite of her not to bid his parents farewell.

Maria and Michael Carlisle solved that particular
problem for her by appearing at the kitchen door.

'I'm sorry it's been almost hello and goodbye,'
apologised Maria Carlisle. 'But I'm sure we'll meet
again. Until then, *que tengas suerte*, Sophie.'

'Knowing my son, I'll second that,' her husband
said with a chuckle. 'And you make sure you take
care of those eyes,' he added sympathetically, giving
her a cheery wave as they both disappeared.

'Ah, there you are!' exclaimed Patrick, entering the
kitchen some while after his parents had left.

Sophie's look was one of complete bewilderment
as he made straight for the fridge, opened its door
and squatted before it to examine the contents.

She had expected...what exactly *had* she expected,
she asked herself distractedly—a sudden, uncharacteristic rush of confidences from him? And why on
earth was she tying herself up in knots over what she
had witnessed? There was probably a score of women
in his life and for all she knew he greeted every one
of them with similar enthusiasm. Feeling inexplicably
comforted by that thought, she dismissed the entire
episode from her mind.

'What does *que tengas suerte* mean?' she asked out
of the blue, uncertain whether or not she had repeated the strange sounds accurately.

'It means good luck,' he replied with obvious
amusement as he swung shut the door and
straightened. 'We'd better make out a list of what food
we'll need—there's hardly anything here.'

Sophie flashed him a look of startled disbelief. 'Surely your stomach can last out till we get to the airport?' she exclaimed, hesitating as his brows rose in questioning arches. 'I mean...we are going back to London...aren't we?'

'Whatever gave you that idea?'

'Your parents aren't here——'

'I'd already told you they wouldn't be,' he interrupted, patience patronisingly exaggerated in his tone.

'But this apartment...it's...it's...' she floundered.

'It's being decorated—so what?' he stated dismissively. 'They won't be touching my room—and you'll be able to use the kitchen.'

'*I'll* be able to use the kitchen?' she exploded.

'I had the feeling you weren't too impressed by my culinary efforts,' he retorted, turning away with a small, eloquently dismissive shrug.

'You're being deliberately obtuse,' she accused. 'Why can't you just admit to having made a mistake?'

'Explain my mistake to me and I'll see if I can oblige,' he countered infuriatingly, giving his full attention to the percolator he was now refilling.

'Coming here, for heaven's sake! You obviously didn't bargain on the place being virtually uninhabitable.'

'It's perfectly habitable. I've told you—my room is——'

'Your room!' she shrieked, her last shreds of patience deserting her. 'You can't possibly imagine I'd agree to share your room with you!'

'Carlisle, with your predilection for impersonating a banshee—and with such convincing brilliance—I can even imagine sharing my bed with you without my self-control being taxed in the slightest. So for God's sake stop screeching at me, you're beginning to give me a headache. Would you like some coffee?' he finished disconcertingly.

It was the unconcerned grin accompanying his words that pricked the bubble of her fury, leaving her feeling curiously deflated while at the same time thoroughly exasperated.

'Yes, please,' she muttered defeatedly, having successfully resisted a powerful urge to ask if he also managed to reduce other women to gibbering fury with such ease. 'Patrick—we *have* to discuss this,' she added, annoyed to hear a note almost of pleading in her words.

'I can sleep in my dressing-room—if that's what's bothering you—until one of the others is ready,' he stated, his eyes narrowing impatiently as she let out an incoherent squeak of protest. 'After all I've said on the subject, I certainly didn't expect to have to repeat that seducing you is the very last of my intentions. And before you start screeching at me again,' he continued coldly as she opened her mouth to retort, 'had that been my intention, I can see no earthly reason why you should imagine I'd drag you all the way here to do so...when all I had to do was let things take their natural course in London.'

'You are utterly despicable!' she shrieked, hurling the nearest thing to hand at him—an empty bread basket.

'Only when I'm needled,' he murmured, swiftly catching the hand that had reached for a small earthenware jug with the intention of sending it flying after the bread basket.

'I wasn't implying I thought you'd brought me here for any ulterior motive,' she snapped, her cheeks aflame as she wrenched free her hand. 'I dare say, from what I've seen, you have plenty of willing candidates here, and anyway—as you so chivalrously pointed out—I'd have been a complete walk-over in London!' She gave a sharp cry of protest as she was grabbed by the shoulders and hauled to her feet.

'No more of a walk-over than I'd have been,' he stated, his words surprisingly gentle, given the harsh grasp of his hands on her shoulders. 'Sophie, I'm sorry I spoke to you like that—you're right, it was utterly despicable.' He released her. 'Come on, tell me I'm forgiven and I'll pour the coffee.'

'It's not a question of forgiving you,' she muttered deflatedly, horrified by her rash reference to what she had witnessed earlier—a reference to which he seemed mercifully oblivious. 'And I don't care how irrational it sounds, but I wish someone could wave a wand and return my life to normal. It just seems as though it's becoming more bizarre with each passing day.' She glared accusingly at him. 'Despite all your charitable words about our being quits, I *am* indebted to you. And I *do* want to give what help I can...but you seem determined not to let me. I know I can't possibly expect you to put me in the picture after my blunder in London—and it *was* a blunder—but...' Her eyes widened in sudden horror. 'Oh, God! That's why they tried to take Fred and José out of police custody!'

'Perhaps you'd feel better on your knees—or prostrate, even—while you metaphorically flagellate yourself,' he observed mildly, placing two cups of coffee on the table and taking the chair beside hers.

'Why do you always have to be so damned sarcastic?' she accused hotly. 'I was merely trying to explain that, though your reluctance to tell me anything tends to drive me mad, I can quite understand it.' She took a quick gulp of coffee in an effort to compose herself, wincing as the hot liquid scalded her throat.

'Well, you can dispense with the sackcloth and ashes as I'm virtually certain your indiscretion in London had no bearing on events in Gamborra. Perhaps you'd like me to take an oath on that...sorry, that *was* sarcastic.'

The look Sophie gave him was a paradoxical mixture of gratitude and resentment.

'Carlisle, of course you're finding it a strain—we both are. It's only to be expected when circumstances force a couple of strangers to live virtually in one another's pockets,' he pointed out quietly. 'I'm probably not the easiest of people to live with at the best of times...and these most certainly can't be described as the best.'

'But you're under far more strain than I am!' she exclaimed, guilt dissipating her anger. 'And all I seem to do is fly off the handle every five minutes.' Not that his making no attempt to deny his reluctance to explain what was going on was offering her any incentive to mend her ways, she realised frustratedly.

'Well, for your penance you can write out the shopping list.' He grinned. 'There's a pen and pad next to the toaster.'

Determined to make every effort to keep the peace, she fetched both, returning to her seat only to stare down blankly at the pad. 'I've no idea what you...we need.'

'Food.'

'Very clever!' she snapped, then, striving to keep calm, added, 'It's just that I'm not familiar with Spanish food.'

'Carlisle, nobody's asking you to go native!' he exclaimed impatiently, taking the pen and pad from her.

'You're deliberately twisting what I said!'

'Milk, potatoes, fruit,' he chanted, ignoring her accusation as his brow creased in concentration. 'Vegetables . . . we could have chops, or a steak tonight.' His glance caught hers, his eyes twinkling teasingly. 'I'm sure you can cook up a masterpiece with basics like that.'

'Still banking on my doing the cooking, I see,' she retorted, a reluctant gleam in her own eyes as she grudgingly acknowledged the breathtaking skill with which he could use humour as a goad.

'I'll quite happily do the cooking,' he murmured innocently. 'It's just that the episode with the omelette——'

'OK, I'll cook,' she conceded exasperatedly. 'But only because I've a nasty suspicion you'd not be above bludgeoning my taste buds until I did.'

'What a *very* nasty, *very* suspicious mind you have,' he observed piously, returning his attention to the list before him.

He resumed writing, dark locks of hair falling untidily across his forehead as he bent his head. Sophie watched in silence, the inexplicable thought entering her mind that he was decidedly not what could be termed photogenic. He looked great on camera, but in the flesh . . . no, the cameras most certainly didn't do him full justice. And as for the length and sweep of those eyelashes, she mused with a small stab of envy, they were nothing short of outrageous. Her eyes

had for some time been taking their leisurely stock of
the finely chiselled planes of his face when she became
conscious of being observed.

'Carlisle, have I just sprouted a third eye or have
you lapsed into a trance?'

'Sorry! I ...I was thinking,' she stammered, hot
colour flooding her cheeks.

'Well, give the thinking a rest and pay attention,'
he ordered, an indefinable something in the eyes momentarily holding hers only deepening her colour.
'Now—the Spanish for milk is——' He broke off,
frowning in concentration, then shook his head. 'No,
it's probably best if I write down what you'll have to
say.' He began writing once more. 'You can read it
back to me and I'll correct your accent.' He gave a
beam of satisfaction. 'Spanish pronunciation is a
doddle—it's completely phonetic.'

Sophie gazed at him blankly. Had she been so completely lost in drooling over his looks that she had
missed something vital he had said?

'And while you're out getting the shopping, I
can——'

'Me?' she squeaked uncomprehendingly. 'Out
getting the shopping?'

'Yes. It's quite simple, all you have to do is——'

'Without you?'

'All on your lonesome, Carlisle.'

'Patrick, I can't possibly! I don't know the place...I
don't speak a word of the language!'

'But I've already told you——'

'Why can't you go? Why can't we both go?'

'Because I'm expecting a phone call.'

'We could go after,' she said, relieved. 'Shops in
Spain stay open quite late, don't they?'

'Yes, but I've no idea what time the call might come. I can't even say with certainty that I'll be getting one.'

Sophie opened her mouth to make a suitably sarcastic remark, then quickly closed it, remembering just in time her resolution to keep the peace, especially while, as on the one hand she could could hardly blame him for refusing to tell her anything, on the other she had a niggling suspicion he was not above manipulating to his own ends any guilt and ignorance on her part ... he even had her agreeing to do the cooking, hadn't he?

'Anyway, there's no problem,' he announced, rising. 'I can order this over the phone—they'll deliver within the hour.' He began moving towards the door, then turned. 'Though I must say I'm most surprised that someone who could swan off to darkest Africa the way you did would chicken out of tackling a place as civilised as Madrid.'

He had disappeared through the door by the time her hand had reached the jug and prepared to take aim. She hastily returned it to the table, horrified by the violence with which her good intentions had been swept aside. She was behaving in a way she would never have dreamed possible, she chided herself in stunned perplexity. She should be keeping firmly in mind the almost intolerable strain under which he was living ... not hurling things at him like a deranged prima donna. There was undoubtedly a very good reason for their being here, even though she had no idea what it was. And it was despicable of her even to question his motives in these circumstances. From now on she was determined to turn over a new leaf, to try to offer him at least something by way of mental support at a time when he must desperately need it.

It was all very well her making good resolutions, argued Sophie frustratedly with herself, stepping out of the bath and angrily towelling her glowing body dry, and altogether another matter actually carrying them out.

Wrapping the towel around her, she made her way into the adjoining bedroom and was immediately having to stifle a gasp of indignation.

'I don't know why you stormed off like that,' complained Patrick from his position prone on the bed which he had allegedly allocated to her.

Sophie began mentally counting to ten. Not only was he in the room and on the bed, but he too had obviously bathed or showered. The dark head nestling on the pillow she was to use glistened not so much with dampness as with out and out wetness, obvious patches of which had darkened the blue of the bathrobe in which he was lounging with such a proprietorial air on the duvet—which too was showing ominously similar patches.

'Would you mind getting off the bed, you're making it wet?' she muttered stiffly. 'And, for the record, I didn't storm off. I . . . I just——'

'Stormed off,' he finished obligingly, displaying that same infuriating smugness which had, if she were completely honest, sent her storming from the kitchen. 'Look, Carlisle, I realise that being forced to camp in the kitchen doesn't exactly constitute the lap of luxury——'

'I'm not demanding luxury!'

'And I also realise how frustrating it must be for you not to be able to understand a word of what's being said on the television——'

'I didn't find it in the least frustrating,' she contradicted acidly, wondering if he had actually forgotten having offered her the use of his room and the bed on which he was now so comfortably—not to mention damply—sprawled. 'It's just that when you suggested giving me a Spanish lesson, I'd no idea I'd be expected to achieve fluency in ten seconds flat! And I also happen to resent being spoken down to as though I were some sort of moronic child.'

'Perhaps I'm just a lousy teacher,' he stated, his tone openly sceptical of so ludicrous an idea. 'But I honestly can't see why the fact that Spanish happens to have two verbs "to be" should tax your mental powers to the extent it obviously does.'

'Probably because—to quote you—you're such a lousy teacher,' she retaliated hotly—he was unspeakable! 'An eight-year-old could have explained it more intelligibly.'

'I dare say—the intellect of an eight-year-old being roughly on a par with yours.' Though his lazy grin took much of the sting from his words, there was something approaching insolence in the eyes casually surveying her towel-clad figure, reminding her more pointedly than any words of her virtual state of undress. 'You'll just have to learn to accept that trading insults with me will always leave you the loser, Carlisle. But never mind——'

They both froze as the distant ring of a telephone cut through his taunting words.

Then he was on his feet, his face tense and pale as he dashed from the room.

Shedding the towel and struggling into her dressing-gown, Sophie raced after him. Uncertain which of the many huge, high-ceilinged rooms she was in, she was stumbling her way around white-shrouded shapes, her only light that petering in from the hallway, her only guide the staccato harshness of Patrick's voice as it almost pleaded against the mouthpiece.

Then she heard the crash of the receiver back on to its rest and found herself wondering what had possessed her to follow him. Whatever this was about, he had made it perfectly clear he had no intention of discussing it with her.

'We were cut off,' he muttered hoarsely, sinking to a sitting position on the white-sheeted floor and dragging the telephone down beside him. 'It's impossible to tell whether or not it was deliberate.' He hugged his knees to his chest, burying his head in the cushion of his arms.

The expected call was obviously coming from Gamborra, though Sophie found the confusion brought about by that realisation being instantaneously overridden by a powerful, completely irrational urge to kneel beside his dejected figure and to place her arms around those broad shoulders now visibly sagging in uncharacteristic defeat.

'Patrick, I——'

Before the phone had finished screeching out its second summons, the receiver was back in his hand.

'*Dígame.*' There was an explosive harshness in that one word, despite its innate Spanish liquidity.

In the tense, laden silence that followed, Sophie found herself unable to take a breath. Then the words were pouring from him—angry, impatient explosions in Spanish that lasted mere seconds before the receiver was returned yet again to its rest.

For several seconds the only sound in the shadowed dimness of the room was the soft rasp of his breathing—quickened as though from physical exertion.

Then he broke the silence. 'I'd never have believed anything could get to me quite like this,' he muttered wearily. 'You're right—I'm turning into a monster.'

This time she found herself hugging her arms across her chest, so powerful was their urge to offer comfort. 'You're no monster—no matter what I may have said in one of my childish fits of temper.' Still hugging her arms to her, she sat on the arm of the sheeted chair nearest him. 'You care very deeply about your friends and it's only natural that you'll now and then give way to the strain you're under.'

'But the close friend I've just been so abominably rude to couldn't have been expected to know this was the worst possible time to choose to call me . . . I'd no right to behave as I did.'

'Perhaps not, but it is very late—hardly a time to be making social calls, wouldn't you say?' she soothed. As she saw his dismissive shake of the head, it suddenly occurred to her that she had absolutely no idea what time it actually was.

'No,' he sighed. 'Anna often rings me far later than this, she knows the sort of hours I keep . . . she was probably expecting me to ring her earlier with my version of what my parents told her on the way to the airport,' he added almost to himself.

So her name was Anna, thought Sophie, conscious of a most unpleasant sensation niggling at her somewhere in the region of her stomach. 'I'm sure she'll understand when you get the chance to explain.'

He lifted his head and looked up at her, a wry smile softening the tense set of his features. 'Don't you start going all soft and understanding on me, Carlisle,' he teased softly. 'I happen to need—how was it you put it?—those childish fits of temper of yours to keep me on the rails ... and I have been behaving very badly,' he added, as her spirits inexplicably lifted and, the unpleasant sensation gone, she gave him a jokingly warning prod in the ribs with her bare foot. 'It's true! I haven't even got around to explaining to you what's going on.'

'You don't have to,' she told him quietly. 'Honestly.'

'Oh, but I want to—honestly,' he teased, then the tension returned to his face. 'When my father rang me in London, it was to tell me that José had rung here.'

Sophie gave a small gasp of shock.

'He and Fred had tried ringing London, only to find all directly dialled calls being intercepted. They then tried this number, merely on the off chance, and got through. Of course there's no guarantee they'll have access to a phone again, but my father promised them there would always be someone here just in case ... in fact, had he not got hold of me, he would have cancelled going to Ireland.'

'And you think it was Fred and José trying to get through just now?' asked Sophie.

He shrugged. 'It's no more than a gut feeling, but yes, I do.'

It was on the tip of Sophie's tongue to point out he could hardly sit by the phone all night until she realised that was probably precisely his intention.

'It would have made life a darn sight easier if my dear mother hadn't decided to have these wretched decorators in!' he exclaimed frustratedly. He gave a small laugh at the sight of Sophie's bewildered reaction to his words. 'There are usually extension phones dotted all over the apartment. Obviously my mother decided they'd only be in the way of the decorators—though heaven only knows where she's stashed them away.' He got to his feet. 'I'd better start searching. And you'd best get some sleep.' He drew her to her feet, grinning as he turned her in the direction of the door. 'Don't worry, I'll be as quiet as a mouse and the flex—if I manage to track down an extension—should just about stretch into my dressing-room.'

'Are you sure you wouldn't like me to help you look?' asked Sophie.

His answer was to give her a firm push towards the door. 'No, off to bed! And I warn you, if you turn out to be a snorer there will be hell to pay!'

CHAPTER SEVEN

HAVING plumped up her pillow for the umpteenth time, Sophie lay back against it. Her mind was alive with an infuriatingly stimulating welter of thoughts at a time when she wanted it empty and relaxed for sleep.

Perhaps it was the subconscious realisation that she would sooner or later be disturbed that was keeping her mind so exhaustingly active, she rationalised. Patrick was hardly the quietest of people, and he would have to come through this room to get to his. And even if he didn't turn on the light, he would still disturb her scrabbling around looking for the telephone point. On the other hand, he might not even find a phone, she reasoned pessimistically, and she would end up awake all night! And she was exhausted. Perhaps not so much physically as mentally—in fact, there were few things she could think of more mentally exhausting than day-to-day living in the company of Patrick! Yet now she had difficulty remembering a time when he had not been part of her life, she realised, turning and burying her face in the pillow as the thought also occurred to her how unimaginably empty life was going to seem without his constant presence.

But there was Anna. And she might as well be honest with herself and admit that the name for what she had experienced at the sight of Anna in Patrick's arms was jealousy—plain and simple. So now what?

As though in answer to that despondent question came words that seemed to have taken up permanent residence in the fringes of her mind since he had first uttered them. 'It's gloves off between us as far as I'm concerned, once this wretched marriage has been annulled.' They were the words of a man who was heart-free, she told herself, examining them with ruthless detachment. No, they were certainly not the sort of words a man committed to another would utter. She had over-reacted, and grossly, to what was probably no more than an exuberant greeting between old friends.

Comforted by her own rational powers of deduction, she found her thoughts taking a disconcerting side-step and she was suddenly reliving the inciting sensation of his lips on hers and the devastating intensity of the passion flaring hotly between them. Then she was back to plumping her pillow in a frantic effort to escape the vivid persistence of those devastatingly provocative thoughts.

She had been feeling so strange—totally unlike herself—for so long now...perhaps Sister Magda's sedatives *had* had some hitherto undetected and ghastly side-effect...the way she was feeling, it was as though she had been turned into some sort of raving nymphomaniac!

More like a raving lunatic, she remonstrated with herself, and, if she would only stop shying away from the facts, there was a good deal more than mere physical desire in her mixed-up feelings towards Patrick. Argumentative and provoking, and every other infuriating thing he might be—the fact was, she liked him. She admired the unstinting loyalty he showed towards his friends, the humanity in him that had resulted in his marrying her.

She turned once more, this time her body surprisingly heavy with incipient sleep. All in all, she desperately loved the wretched man . . . and therein lay the source of just about every problem plaguing her.

Had it not been for her momentary feelings of complete disorientation in the instant the distant ringing of a telephone returned her to consciousness, Sophie would have sworn that the last thing she would have been capable of doing was sleeping.

But sleeping she had been, she knew, as awareness returned to her in a sudden surge of panic, propelling her from the warm security of her bed and sending her racing blindly towards the urgent sound of Patrick's voice.

He must have been cut off again, she thought, sick with disappointment for him as, what seemed like no time after she had sped into the room, he replaced the receiver.

'That was José,' he stated wearily, surprising her with his awareness of her presence.

'You actually spoke to him?' she exclaimed breathlessly, skirting the shrouded mounds of furniture and sinking to the floor beside him.

'There was one hell of a storm going on—which caused the problem earlier on too—I could only just hear him,' he muttered, dragging his fingers through his hair in a gesture of utter weariness. 'They've had to travel by night because of the patrols . . . and then not every night because of the rains.'

'But they're still free,' coaxed Sophie. Perhaps it was the dimness of the light, but he looked drawn—haggard almost.

'Yes, they're still free,' he echoed tonelessly. 'They'll be travelling through the bush from now on till they reach Zambia.'

'How long do you think that will take?'

He shrugged. 'Two—maybe three days...I've really no idea. They won't be ringing again until they're safely over the border.'

'That sounds very positive, they——'

'What's so positive about it?' he interrupted harshly. 'They're still on the run...they still could be picked up between now and making it to the border.' He lifted his head, his gaze chilling.

'But there's far less likelihood of their being caught in the bush regions.' Sophie continued earnestly, troubled by his unrelenting pessimism.

He hesitated, then his eyes softened. 'What would I do without you, Carlisle?' he sighed ruefully, reaching out a hand and gently ruffling her hair. 'You have an admirable knack of managing to point out the glaringly obvious at those times when my mind refuses to see it.'

'I can understand why your mind would be having problems at the moment,' she told him, conscious of the warm weight of his hand as it slid to her shoulder. 'When did you last sleep?'

He removed his hand abruptly. 'Don't, for God's sake, start trying to mother me,' he snapped. 'Because——'

'For your information, I don't feel in the least inclined to mother you,' retorted Sophie hotly, deeply

resentful of the inexplicable harshness of his words.
'You can damn well——'

'Sophie—please!' Suddenly she was in his arms, his
mouth hot and insistent on hers, parting her trembling, welcoming lips in a fervid, plundering search.

She clung to him, responding unrestrainedly to an
instant and overwhelming need erupting in her as
knowledge and acceptance of the totality of her love
for him filled her.

'Sophie, I have to keep goading you...fighting you,'
he breathed raggedly, his mouth a moist heat burning
on her skin as it moved downwards to nuzzle in small
frantic kisses against her throat. 'It's the only way I
can fight what you do to me. But tonight...Sophie,
there's no fight left in me tonight. Tonight, let me
keep you here in my arms.'

'I don't want you to fight,' she shivered softly, the
words torn from her as his hands swept slowly and
sensuously down the length of her body, then back,
deftly removing the nightgown from her. 'Patrick, I...'
Her words became lost in a startled cry of need as his
hands began retracing their journey, their gentle
sureness as they weaved their tantalising butterfly way
sending sharp jolts of awareness jarring through her
till there was no part of her at peace.

'Sophie, you're my madness,' he groaned desperately. 'My beautiful, irresistible madness.'

She tried to speak, but the words refused to come
as the ache in her grew to a craving for far more than
the inflammatory weightlessness of his touch—a
craving that became her own irresistible madness as
that tantalising touch played on against her body,
darkening the rosiness from the nipples over which
they skimmed, leaving them sharp nuggets of desire

as her body arched in trembling eagerness towards his.

A small cry of protest escaped her as he drew away from her, impatiently shrugging free of his robe. Then he reached for her once more, his hands sliding down her back, folding across the firm swell of her buttocks as he suddenly drew her body against the length of his.

Need then became a mindless dictator within her, bringing soft panting cries from her bursting lungs as her body became no longer hers to command, glorying wantonly in the sheer force of physical arousal it encountered in the lean, taut strength of his.

Then there was no longer that maddening gentleness in his hands; there was an assurance and purpose in their touch, a strength that commanded, a confidence that forewarned of the abundant power of the magic they could wreak.

'Sophie, tell me you don't want me to stop... that you want me as I want you,' he groaned softly, his hips a sensuous sway against hers as those sure hands manipulated her body, moulding it to the fiercely throbbing heat of his before rising to her breasts where the tinglingly exciting rasp of his chest hairs became replaced by the inflaming exploration of probing fingers. 'Tell me, Sophie,' he urged, his hands cupping her breasts, their fingers splaying in their restless, searching caress.

'You must know how I want you!' she cried out, her head twisting from side to side in frantic, silent protest at the madness of sensation being inflicted upon her body. 'Patrick, please...'

Yet even as those hands ceased their exquisite torture and his arms locked convulsively around her, there was still that madness-inducing message in the slow, sensuous rhythm of his hips against hers, of promises being made yet still unfulfilled. Then his fingers were sinking into her hair, drawing back her head as his mouth lowered to her throat, his breath a hot, inciting sweetness against her flesh as the moist trail of his murmuring, searching mouth ended at the taut swell of her breasts.

The cry that exploded from her was one in which longing had reached the borders of pain when that relentlessly exploring mouth opened against her breast, its moist heat tensing and swelling her flesh as though to bursting-point as his probing tongue played like an instrument of exquisite torture against the taut sharpness of her nipple.

Where before her hands had remained passive, now the ache of need throbbing through her entire body goaded them into abandoning their fluttering uncertainty as that ache became magnified beyond all endurance. In a purely reflex action her hands raked across his back, gaining confidence from the sharp tensing of the muscles rippling beneath them, revelling in the softly shuddered moan their trespass brought. Then they were exploring, sliding to the hollow of his back where her fingers found the silky softness of down-like hair, faltering only when trapped by the uncontrollable trembling now racking her entire body—a trembling that grew till there was no part of her not ensnared in its shuddering hold.

'It's all right,' he whispered, gathering her tormented body gently to him. And she clung to him, the severity of her shaking only increasing as her body responded with complete abandon to the virile nakedness of his, her hips moulding to the heat of his, her legs entwining and luxuriating against the silken-haired sensation of his.

'Sophie, relax,' he pleaded unsteadily, striving to still the shivering body now moving with ever-growing abandon against his.

'I can't,' she choked, her hands locking round his neck, her body unable to respond to the impossible. 'Patrick ... please!'

His hands eased her, moving her fully on to her back.

'Yes,' he promised huskily, a single frail shaft of moonlight filtering its way through the darkness to bathe his face in its ghostly silver sheen as his body began gently guiding hers. 'Put your arms around my neck,' he whispered urgently.

She lifted her arms in obedience, a breathless, waiting suspension mesmerising her as she felt first the firm, purposeful guidance of his legs against hers, then the acute tension gripping the lean body poised in sudden stillness above hers.

Then his name was a cry of welcome on her lips as his hands moved, lifting her to receive him. The second cry that was wrung from her was one that choked from shock to startled pleasure with the swift, almost savagely exultant completeness with which his body plundered hers.

And that one instinctive instant of shock was lost in the melting warmth suddenly exploding in rapturous, riotous excitement within her as her hands raked compulsively against his glistening torso and her body abandoned itself to his without reserve.

Soft, unintelligible words whispered on his lips as his body took control, gradually slowing hers to a rhythm of torment and pleasure beyond the capacity

of any dream. His was an invasion that fanned the
heat within her to a furnace, gathering up hot pools
of pleasure within her and sending her senses crashing
around her as each pool swelled to a raging torrent
of rapture in which she could only drown.

And even as she drowned she was rejoicing in this
ultimate expression of her love—drowning and rejoicing while the cries spilling from her incited a new
urgency, a growing wildness, in the body wrapping
her in its web of enchantment. It was there in the
frenzied quest of his mouth, biting its rage of passion
against the soft curve of her neck—in the heat within
her that swept her along, leading her towards the impossible with the wild insistence of its drive, keeping
her hovering on the edge of oblivion till his sharp cry
of exultation carried her over that edge and the love
within her was erupting in a force that tore through
her, buffeting and tossing her until fulfilment came
in an exploding ecstasy that was total enchantment.

She clung to him in a haze of uncomprehending
joy, drowsily conscious of the same sensuous spasms
of contentment shivering through him as did through
her, while his soft groans subsided to murmurs and
those murmurs became husky sighs of endearment
from lips that panted softly against the smooth white
curve of her throat.

While the crazy pounding of her heart slowly subsided to an erratic thud, his soft, unintelligible Spanish
words washed gently around her ears. They had to be
words of love, she told herself dreamily. What else
could they be, when there was no name other than
love for what they had just shared?

She reached up, running her fingers through the
heavy rich darkness of his hair, luxuriating in its

springy, silken feel, part of her mind striving to collect her scattered senses while another begged silently for him to translate those soft words still sighing intermittently from his lips. Her own words of love jostled impatiently within her, awaiting only those from him that would provide the key to their release.

'You seem such a tiny thing,' he murmured, a soft edge of regret in his voice as he gently eased his weight from her and in doing so broke the last intimate ties of passion. 'So perfect, yet somehow so tiny,' he whispered, turning to his side and enfolding her gently in his arms.

Though she strove to smother the rage of disappointment racking her, the slightly abrasive sensation of his chest hairs against her naked breasts warned her of the shuddering sigh that had escaped her. She had been holding her breath, she thought, a terrible, lethargic sadness ploughing destructively through the last shreds of her joy. She had held her breath in anticipation of his words of love. But it had been his body alone loving her with such total commitment—his heart had not participated.

'Are you sleepy?' he whispered, his fingers searching against her face then gently tracing the outline of her mouth.

She nodded, not trusting herself to speak.

'We'll talk later,' he stated, leaving her wondering if she had imagined a faint tinge of relief colouring his words as she later listened to the gentle easing of his breathing towards sleep.

She closed her eyes, the riotous abandonment of her joy now only a ghostly memory beneath the all-encompassing blanket of the sadness now smothering her. There would be no words of love—not from

Patrick. What he had shared with her had been no more than a physical expression of the desire that had simmered between them almost from the start—a desire he had always candidly acknowledged as no more than an amusing inconvenience.

She gave a small shiver of horror at the memory of reckless words of love that had come so close to pouring from her, and as she reacted, so did he, his arms tightening protectively around her, fanning the love that lay trapped in silence within her to a raging furnace of despair.

She awoke in her own bed to the soft gleam of sunlight filtering out like a halo from behind the heavy fullness of the curtains. She swung her legs over the side of the bed, a harsh tremor of awareness jolting through her at the realisation of her nakedness.

Vague, half-formed memories returned to her, of his lifting her and carrying her to this room. Her fingers rose involuntarily to lips that felt strangely full—bruised almost. Had it been her imagination, or had his mouth lingered in the softness of a kiss on hers when he had drawn the quilt over her?

But the savage force of the memories jarring through her as she showered and dressed had nothing to do with imagination, she thought despairingly, battling to smother the stomach-churning excitement with which her body so uninhibitedly responded to the relentless bombardment of those memories.

One thing was certain, she couldn't face him in this state, she told herself agitatedly, sitting down on the edge of the bed and clenching her hands into fists in an effort to still their trembling.

What would he say? For that matter, what would she say? How could she possibly be feeling like this? Last night she had made love with the man she now knew she loved beyond all reason, yet he had left her to sleep alone; and now her heart was pounding and she was feeling almost physically sick at the thought of facing him, she thought bewilderedly. Hardly the stuff dreams were made of, she reminded herself in a listless attempt to pull herself together, then froze at the sound of a rap on the door.

'Sophie, are you up?'

'Yes.' Her pulses raced out of control.

'The decorators are here, so we'd best breakfast out. Is that OK with you?'

'Fine—I'll be with you in a moment.' Her hands were now shaking so violently that she shoved them in the pockets of the pale lilac cotton dress she was wearing, then took a deep breath and marched out of the room before the last shreds of her courage deserted her.

Patrick was in the kitchen, his tall, lean body rocking almost imperceptibly back and forth as he stood by the sink, his thumbs hooked in the pocket vents of immaculately cut dark trousers while he gazed through the window and down on to the cobble-stoned, plant-strewn courtyard below.

'I'm ready,' she said quietly, slipping her darkened glasses on over eyes unable to get their fill of him.

He gave a slight start, then turned. 'Sophie, are you...?' He hesitated, the sunlight dancing across the breadth of his shoulders forcing her to lower her gaze before she could attempt reading his. 'Are you all right?'

'Yes, I'm all right. I'm fine,' she stated. 'Let's go, I'm starving.' She had no idea from where she had produced those breezy words—so calm, so completely without trace of her inner turmoil—but she gained a small measure of confidence from them, as she did also from the momentary shock that fleetingly ruffled the guarded composure of his features.

'There's a bar not too far from here—I often use it.' Almost without pausing for breath, he called out to the workmen, walking past her and out into the hall as he did so.

'Did I misunderstand or did you say we were going to a bar?' she asked, following him out of the relatively cool darkness of the building and into the blinding brightness of morning sunlight.

'There's a world of difference between a Spanish and an English bar...oh, hell, I didn't think!' he exclaimed as he noticed her problem and immediately shielded her from the glare with his body. 'This light is far too strong for you.'

She shook her head. 'No. It'll just take me a few moments to adjust.' Again her tone was comfortingly calm, but his obvious concern was threatening to undo any benefit she derived from that fact. His was a concern he would show for anyone, she kept reminding herself as her eyes gradually adjusted...it was his capacity for concern that had led him into marrying her!

She concentrated determinedly on their surroundings—on the tall, stately trees standing guard around buildings of old-world charm and beauty. Then she gave a gasp of pure disbelief as they reached the end of the side-street down which he had led her and stepped into the chaos of a capital city in the throes of its rush hour.

'This is unbelievable!' she exclaimed. 'And I didn't realise it had been raining!'

He glanced down at her, the ghost of a smile hovering on his lips. 'It hasn't been raining—they hose the streets down every morning. Welcome to Madrid.'

That ghost of a smile only served to underline how tense he looked, she realised with a mixture of anger and sadness, futilely wishing she could put back the clock—not because she had regrets but because he so obviously had.

'I should warn you, Spanish and English breakfasts are as different as their bars,' he told her, catching hold of her arm and steering her through an open doorway in the bustling, thronging street.

Sophie was aware of the crush around her and the hubbub of voices, but her eyes flatly refused to rush their adjustment to the sudden dimness. She felt Patrick's arm catch her as she stumbled blindly against something, then its firm guidance as he steered her past the crush of people lining the bar and into a secluded booth.

'Sophie, are you sure you're all right?' he asked anxiously as she gingerly felt her way along the wooden table before lowering herself on to the cushioned seat.

'I'm fine—it's just that I'd barely got used to the light and now we're back in darkness.'

He sat down opposite her and her heart fell as she slipped off her glasses and saw the guarded tension drawn on his features. The truth of the matter was that he was embarrassed, she told herself, the realisation filling her with a humiliation that only fuelled her now hotly smouldering anger. How dared he? And what was more, how dared he be so unspeakably boorish as to show it?

'About breakfast——'

'As long as it doesn't entail anything alcoholic, I'm sure I'll cope.' Just as long as she kept her cool, warned an inner voice.

'We usually have milky coffee and pastries...or there's chocolate, but you might find that rather rich.'

'I'll try the chocolate,'she said, responding with childish fervour to a feeling that he was not recommending it.

'*Churros y chocolate,*' he told the waiter who had just appeared and smilingly greeted him by name.

'I thought you were having coffee,' muttered Sophie.

'No, breakfast is about the only time I have a sweet tooth,' he replied evenly.

She compressed her lips, but said nothing, battling with alien feelings of aggression—of violence, almost. How could she possibly have squandered her love on a man who, having made love to her with such passionate abandon one moment, could feel no more than acute embarrassment the next? Breakfast? How could she even contemplate breakfast when she felt positively sick with humiliation?

'Patrick, I——'

'Sophie——'

Their simultaneous words were silenced by the arrival of the waiter bearing large glasses nestling in glazed ceramic holders and a dish of what looked to Sophie like finger-shaped doughnuts.

'You dunk the *churros* in the chocolate,' he told her, picking up a pastry and dipping it in his drink.

For a moment Sophie contemplated hurling both the dish and her drink at him. It was her vivid imagination of the likely repercussions of such an action that caused her to give a mental shrug and follow suit. The chocolate coated and clung thickly to the pastry, and both seemed to melt in perfection in her mouth as she took a bite.

'It's delicious!' she exclaimed, the words escaping her before she could harness them.

'You're not supposed to drip the chocolate all over yourself, Carlisle,' he groaned, a smile softening his features as he grabbed a snowy white napkin and wiped her chin with it. Then, as though suddenly coming to his senses, his hand froze and he replaced the napkin on the table, his expression reverting to its former guarded tenseness.

He had inadvertently relaxed for a moment ... he had called her Carlisle. All those times she had complained about his referring to her by his surname, she thought numbly, and now her heart had leapt in welcome to it as though to a caress. How cringe-makingly pathetic!

'Sophie, I realise I'm handling this appallingly,' he muttered, gazing moodily into his drink.

'Handling *what* appallingly?' she asked, control deserting her.

'When I think of how irresponsibly I behaved last night——'

'You?' she butted in, unable to believe her ears. 'How dare you speak as though I'm some sort of mindless creature who has no say in what happens to me?'

'Sophie, that's not what I meant——'

'Well, that's exactly how it sounds,' she cut in, her voice tight with rage.

'Sophie, there are certain responsibilities a man has——'

'And not a woman?' she shrieked. 'Or is what's worrying you the fact that we're technically married? Whatever you think, it wasn't a consummation of the marriage——'

'It damn well was, but——'

'You can say I drugged your drink and had my wicked way with you if it'll make you feel any better!'

'Sophie, stop being so ridiculous! Unless I was very much mistaken, you were a virgin until last night.'

'And the way you're carrying on, anyone would think it had been the other way round! You're pathetic——'

'Damn it, Sophie, would you just shut up long enough for me to——?'

'Why should I? You're a complete wimp——'

'Why?' he demanded, lunging across the table and grasping her by the shoulders. 'Because I feel such deep shame over the fact that for the first time in my life I got so carried away that taking contraceptive precautions didn't even enter my mind?'

'You...I...' Her disjointed attempts at speech petered to silence as he released her and slumped back heavily in his seat.

'It only came to me when you were lying there in my arms...so small...almost childlike.' There was troubled darkness in the eyes that met hers before they widened in sudden understanding. 'And it hadn't entered your mind either, had it, Sophie?' he stated hoarsely. 'Not until this very moment.'

He was right, she thought, almost rigid with shock and the confusing welter of feelings assailing her. Not once in all the tumult of thoughts churning in her mind since her moment of wakening had this—the most pertinent of all—occurred to her.

'Patrick, I...no, it hadn't,' she conceded miserably, shock-waves of reaction still washing through her. 'I...I feel every bit as ashamed as you do—the responsibility was no less mine than it was yours...yet the thought...it never once even entered my mind.'

He reached across the table, covering her clenching hands with his. 'I don't agree—about the responsibility being equally yours—not when it was your first experience of lovemaking.' His hands tightened. 'But if it's a fight you're looking for,' he chided, his tone softening noticeably, 'this wimp doesn't take too kindly to being referred to as pathetic.'

'Patrick, I'm sorry,' she whispered, her cheeks burning. 'I really didn't mean it.'

'No? I'd feel inclined to agree that only the most pathetic of wimps would have had a moment's regret over having made love to a beautiful, enchantingly exciting——' He broke off as she tried to avert her face from the candid scrutiny of his gaze. 'Sophie, it just didn't occur to me that you might not have realised... Hell, you just about blew my libido to smithereens—how could you possibly not have realised what you were doing to me?'

'Smithereens?' she murmured bemusedly, the weight of the world slipping from her shoulders as the rest of her turned to jelly.

'Cut it out, Carlisle,' he warned huskily, raising one of her hands to his lips. 'This is supposed to be mortal combat over your calling me a wimp, not...' The blatant caress in his eyes as his words trailed to a halt sent her senses reeling drunkenly. 'Sophie, can you understand why I'm finding this marriage more and more of a millstone? I want us to be free, so that——' This time his words ended abruptly, and the tension was back in his face as he released her hands.

'Patrick, I think now's the time for us to get the plain speaking over and done with,' stated Sophie firmly, her mind suddenly clear. 'Our first priority, once Fred and José reach Zambia, is to start whatever legal proceedings now necessary to end this marriage—agreed?'

'Sophie, things aren't quite the same——'

'I asked you if you agreed?'

'How can I possibly agree? If you were pregnant——'

'Whatever the odds are, I'm sure they're pretty low, and anyway, that's irrelevant.'

'What the hell do you mean, irrelevant?' he snapped, his expression stubborn and unyielding. 'It's an old wives' tale about it not happening the first time.'

'For heaven's sake, that's not the point!' she exclaimed frustratedly.

'Sophie, what *is* the point?' he demanded harshly. 'We don't know one way or another yet . . . so let's save our breath till we do—agreed?'

'No! Patrick, you——'

'You'll damn well have to agree, because I don't intend discussing it until we have something specific to discuss. That goes for the worrying too. So—do you agree?'

She opened her mouth to disagree, then closed it with a groan of frustration.

'You're learning, Carlisle,' he murmured drily. 'Slowly, but at least you're learning.' He gave her a sudden and completely disarming grin as she glowered disbelievingly at him. 'Now, how about some more chocolate? I think this lot's past its prime.'

CHAPTER EIGHT

IT WAS late by the time they returned to the apartment—so late that Sophie was surprised to find the decorators only then about to leave.

She leaned back against the hall wall, the physical after-effects of the day beginning to catch up on her as she listened to Patrick and one of the men converse. It no longer seemed strange to her to hear the soft, slightly lisping Spanish sounds emanating from him with such total fluency. It was a language she was finding more and more attractive, despite her inability to understand more than the very occasional word.

She settled herself more comfortably against the wall as the two men continued speaking. No wonder she felt so pleasantly spent, she thought, her mind drifting back to her confused surprise when, after their decidedly traumatic breakfast, he had casually suggested showing her the sights of Madrid.

'Sophie, I've already told you, life's too short to spend any of it worrying over a problem that might never exist,' he had said, immediately sensing her reaction.

'But I can't just switch it off,' she had protested, slightly shocked by his seeming ability to do just that. 'And you can't say you weren't worried—this morning you were——'

'I wasn't worried,' he had pointed out brusquely. 'I was wallowing in a purely selfish sense of outrage at having turned out to be every bit as irresponsible as the next man. But I promise you that should the need arise I'll be doing enough worrying for the pair of us—and then some. Now—do you want me to show you Madrid or not?'

Though his *laissez-faire* attitude to life approached the realms of eccentricity by her standards, and was also something she felt incapable of emulating even given a lifetime of practice, she certainly had to admit there were probably few to equal his charm, wit and knowledgeability when playing the role of guide.

'Quality, not quantity,' he had admonished on several occasions, limiting her to four rooms only of the breath-taking wealth of splendour in the famous Prado museum, and steering her ruthlessly past attractions not on his specific agenda.

'I'll take you there another day...' The third time he had made that particular remark, she had given up trying to reason with herself and had unrestrainedly wallowed in the pleasure of his thinking in terms of future days spent with her.

'Sophie, don't you dare go to sleep on me!' Those laughing, teasing words brought her sharply back to the present. 'Don Miguel here has been telling me how his men have worked like demons to get a sitting-room ready for the beautiful *señora* to relax in.' The Spaniard beside him smiled and gave a small bow. 'And as I've told him the only inspection I'm capable of right now is the bathroom ceiling—from a position prone in a tub of hot water—the pair of you are on your own!' With a chuckle and a grinning salute, he promptly left.

Sophie smiled uncertainly at Don Miguel, a distracting and uncomfortable dryness creeping from her throat to her mouth as he beckoned and she reluctantly began following him.

She walked into the room, conscious of a positive leadenness in her feet, then gave a choked gasp of mixed relief and appreciation at the sight that greeted her. With the heavy sheeting now removed to reveal the exquisite formal elegance of the furniture, the room was unrecognisable. It seemed larger—airier and brighter—than she had imagined it would be, the heavy darkness of highly polished wood floors relieved by the pale, muted pastels of several scattered Chinese rugs, and the stark plainness of the walls warmed by the merest hint of cream in their whiteness.

Without being fully aware of it, she had dreaded returning to this room, she realised, feeling almost light-headed with relief.

'It really is beautiful,' she told the man waiting by the door, her tone and the expression of pleasure on her face demolishing all barriers of language.

And it really was beautiful, she told herself, returning to the room once again after seeing the Spaniard out. She sat down on one of two large sofas facing one another, her fingers idly stroking against the cream slubbed silk of the upholstery. Very beautiful, but most impractical, she mused, her body relaxing as tiredness wafted gently through her.

They must have walked miles, she thought, tilting her head back and closing her eyes . . . she could quite happily doze off.

Her head jerked forward, her eyes opening wide with mystification. How could she possibly think in terms of dozing off? She should be prostrate with worry! The possibility that she was pregnant was something that should be dominating her *every* thought, not one she had to dredge up to examine! 'Oh, heck, what's happening to me?' she groaned softly, her body slumping back in defeat as her eyes closed once more. Perhaps Patrick's cavalier attitude to life was rubbing off on her... though the truth was that he was right in saying it was pointless worrying over something that might never materialise. Yet it wasn't so much that she wasn't worrying, she thought confusedly, it was more that her mind seemed to have erected an impermeable wall around the entire subject.

She leapt to her feet the instant the phone rang, grateful for so opportune an interruption. But as she moved towards the two tall windows and the small carved table between them on which the phone now rested, her feet dragged in the hope that Patrick might have heard and be on his way. She waited a further few seconds, then picked up the receiver.

'Hello?' She pulled a small face as a total silence greeted her. Surely they wouldn't have rung off so quickly, she thought guiltily, on the verge of replacing the receiver when a woman's voice, cool yet attractively accented, spoke.

'I wish to speak with Patrick, please.'

'Yes—if you wouldn't mind holding on for a moment, I'll call him,' answered Sophie, the words coming out in a breathless rush.

She sped into the hall. 'Patrick—phone!'

'Who is it?' came his muffled reply.

'I don't know.' Though every spark of intuition she possessed proclaimed it to be Anna, she admitted with reluctance as she made her way to the kitchen and began making a pot of tea.

She picked up the kettle, telling herself she would probably have felt better had she had a definite picture of the woman, instead of just that blurred glimpse of a slim, dark-haired figure...locked in Patrick's arms.

Finding she had filled the kettle to overflowing, she gave a disgusted shake of her head and turned off the tap. Why on earth was she subjecting herself to this ridiculous rigmarole of jealousy when she had already sorted out the entire question of Anna to her own satisfaction?

She plugged in the kettle and leaned against the table, vivid memories of the total lack of inhibition of his passion flooding her, as if to confirm the validity of her painstaking sortings out. Then she found herself gazing glassy-eyed at the kettle, waiting for it to boil and wondering why on earth she should think herself qualified to read anything into the vagaries of men's passions... Discounting Steven, whom she had loved more as a brother, her experiences with men had been little short of disastrous—all two of them. She had ended up in Gamborra virtually to escape the first—Robert—a delightfully engaging Australian doctor who had carelessly omitted to mention a wife back in Melbourne during his ardent courtship of her. What a creep; but how dangerously close she had been to losing her heart to that creep, she thought with disgust. And lo and behold, she had returned from her Gamborran refuge with disaster number two in tow and just raring to happen! And, needless to say, it wasn't the average man in the street with whom she had become embroiled this time, and with whom she had so inconveniently fallen in love. Oh, no, this time she had hit the jackpot and picked on Patrick Carlisle, a man who had otherwise perfectly sane women—her friend Susie Brown being a prime example—glued to their television sets and drooling whenever he appeared on the screen. That the man had undeniable sex appeal was something that hadn't actually struck her until she had met him in the flesh—and then it had virtually pole-axed her.

She heated the teapot, despondently telling herself that all this introspection was leading her nowhere except into the depths of depression. But her thoughts ploughed doggedly on. This man, unfortunately, also happened to have numerous other things going for him besides sex appeal...which was why her loving him as she now did had been so inevitable.

She broke off from her gloomy reveries, startled to find she had gone through all the motions of making the tea without even realising it...yet where had all her profound thinking got her? No further than that she loved a man who enjoyed her company and who found her exceptionally physically attractive...but no more; last night had shown her that.

'Tea—good, just what I need.'

Sophie spun round, her face draining of colour as she caught sight of him taking a seat at the table. 'I...I didn't hear you come in,' she stammered.

'Bare feet,' he grinned, rising and getting the cups. 'You look a bit peaky,' he said, the soft concern in his voice cutting through her like a knife. 'I'm afraid I got carried away dragging you round the city like that.'

'No,' she protested. 'I really enjoyed it—I could have gone on for hours.' She handed him a cup of tea and took her own to the table.

'I'm glad you like it. I suppose I'm prejudiced, having been born here, but it's my favourite of all cities. I know the rush-hour traffic is a nightmare, and the climate lousy——'

'The climate lousy?' echoed Sophie, determined to shake free from her shroud of gloom. 'You call constant warmth and sunshine when it's almost November lousy?'

'Ah, but days like today tend to be the exception,' he smiled. 'Take the word of a true *madrileño*, this city is renowned for being either too hot or too cold. You see, the Castilian plateau on which it's built is over two thousand feet above sea-level, making this the highest capital city in Europe.'

'Well, I've decided I like extremes of weather,' stated Sophie, her gloomy tension easing as she gratefully pounced on that least contentious subject of all—the weather. 'That was the only thing I found dull about Gamborra—its weather, or rather its lack of it,' she explained. 'I arrived almost at the end of the rains, so I missed all the exciting storms. The only difference I could detect between the seasons was that in one it rained for about forty minutes each day and in the other it didn't.'

'But I bet you'll be hankering for a spot of that constant Gamborran sunshine once winter starts to bite,' he laughed, rising. 'More tea?'

She nodded. 'Thanks.'

'You never did get around to telling me what took you to Gamborra in the first place,' he said, filling her cup.

'I trained with a girl from there—Dorothy Shaba,' she began, her thoughts racing. She felt no inclination to bring up Robert—her initial reason for wanting to be as far from London as humanly possible. 'Dorothy was to nurse for a year with the sisters after she had completed her training.'

'If you're as intent on getting as far away from that creep as you say you are,' Dorothy had offered at a time when Sophie had felt her world on the verge of disintegrating around her, 'I know just the place.'

'She really wanted to stay on in London and do a midwifery course, but she didn't want to let the sisters down—so I took her place.'

'Just like that?'

'Just like that,' echoed Sophie, smiling.

Once Dorothy had received confirmation that the sisters would happily accept a substitute, Sophie had found the cause of her spontaneous decision to flee fading rapidly from her thoughts as she had made her excited plans. Her conviction that her heart had been broken, when the matter of Robert's having a wife had come to light, had been well and truly dispelled long before the day of her departure had arrived.

'And your father's reaction?'

'Apoplectic!' In fact, her father had just about run out of words by the time she had informed him of her decision to leave—not that she intended discussing that with Patrick. But apoplectic was a pretty fair description of his reaction to learning his daughter had become involved—albeit unknowingly—with a married man. As though married men had their status tattooed across their foreheads and only crass stupidity prevented a woman from spotting it, she remembered, more with exasperation than bitterness.

'You do give him a hard time,' murmured Patrick, his eyes twinkling with mischief. 'You float off under one dark cloud, then land back under an even bigger and blacker one.'

'Yet he was a lot better disposed to me when I returned than when I left—thanks mainly to you.'

'Thanks nothing to me—the man loves you,' he pointed out gently. 'Both he and your mother were sick with worry by the time I accosted them.' Even as he spoke he was glancing at his watch and rising. 'I'm afraid I have to go out this evening,' he stated, a hint of apology in his tone. 'Will you be OK ... I mean, here on your own?'

'Probably,' she murmured, struggling to keep her face straight. 'Though, to be on the safe side, you'd best take any matches with you—like most children, I tend to play with them.'

'Very droll, Carlisle.' He grinned. 'And I dare say you'll manage to locate a rolling-pin with which to greet me on my return—that being the customary practice among wives, or so I've heard.'

'Not being a wife, I wouldn't know,' she retorted, then immediately decided the statement required qualification. 'Not a proper wife, I mean.' The instant the words were out, instinct and the look he flashed her warned her she should have left well alone. There was the flushed warmth of colour on her cheeks as she quickly gathered up the cups and took them to the sink.

'Being a perverse sort of man, I find the idea of an improper wife infinitely more desirable.'

Sophie trained her eyes resolutely on the sink before her. The small hairs prickling at the back of her neck warned her of his proximity, yet she had been completely unaware of any movement on his part before uttering those teasingly seductive words. Her entire body froze to complete stillness as she felt the momentarily lingering pressure of his lips at the nape of her neck.

'Which makes it more or less imperative that I go out tonight,' he added expressionlessly.

Her every muscle strained almost to breaking-point, Sophie remained unnaturally still as she sensed him move away.

It was only the eventual sound of the front door closing that unlocked her frozen limbs and allowed the breath trapped in her its freedom.

Of course he still wanted her, she intoned silently to herself—but that was all. And no blame could be attached to him for that, because, despite his being a powerfully sensuous man, he was also one of undeniable integrity.

She began rinsing out the cups, her movements wooden and automatic. Perhaps she had expected too much too soon . . . the suddenness, the reckless spontaneity of the love that had so rapidly consumed her, could hardly be described as normal. Perhaps, once the barrier of the marriage between them was gone, there was a chance he could come to love her.

She found herself gazing through the window, down on to the large courtyard below. That morning's vibrant, sun-kissed profusion of colour now lay dimmed in the drabness of the gathering dusk. Yet beauty would be restored with the coming of tomorrow's sun, she thought, willing a spark of hope to ignite in the drab darkness of her own mind. Soon Fred and José would have reached their sanctuary. Soon she would know she was not pregnant . . . she turned from the window, scarcely conscious of the hot rush of tears now scalding her cheeks. Soon the marriage would be over . . . and then, perhaps . . .

*   *   *

She had slept fitfully, merely hovering on the borders of sleep. She had heard him return long after midnight, and then later the sharp ring of the telephone, quickly silenced.

She had more than enough troubles to be going on with, she thought fretfully as she lay there willing sleep to come, without being saddled with insomnia.

Then every nerve in her body jarred to absolute wakefulness as she heard the door open.

'Sophie... are you awake?'

Something in his tone sent her scrabbling to switch on the bedside light. 'Patrick? Is something wrong?' she asked, fear colouring her voice as she struggled upright.

'No—nothing's wrong,' he said. 'I just wanted to——' He broke off, raising his hands to his head and rubbing them against his hair in a gesture so dazed and uncertain that Sophie was on her feet in one instant and beside him in the next, her hands tugging frantically against his raised arms.

'Patrick, are you hurt?' she begged, the words ragged with a sickening fear.

'No...I...I've just had a call from Fred in Zambia. He and José are on their way down to Lusaka.'

'Oh, Patrick!' she cried, flinging her arms around him. 'I can't believe it...it's wonderful! Are they both safe and well?'

'Fred says they are, but I was relieved to hear the Zambians are insisting on giving them a thorough medical going-over once they reach Lusaka.'

'I suppose it's because I wasn't expecting to hear anything for another couple of days that the news is taking so long to sink in!' she exclaimed excitedly, hugging him tightly. 'You gave me such a fright! You

sounded so...I'm not sure how, but it frightened me.'
Before she had finished uttering them, her words had
begun faltering with her sudden realisation of how
tightly locked in each other's arms they now were.

'I didn't mean to frighten you,' he sighed, his arms
tightening compulsively as he began rocking her to
and fro. 'It's just that...hell, I'm having considerable
difficulty not blubbing like a baby!' he groaned disbelievingly, dropping his head to bury his face against
the curve of her shoulder.

'It's perfectly understandable,' she told him gently,
easing free from him and guiding him firmly towards
the bed. 'It's a form of shock...just sit down and
relax.'

'I'm not shocked, damn it!' he growled, dazedly
sitting down. 'I'm delighted.'

'Shock can be caused by nice things as well as nasty,'
she pointed out, the nurse in her taking over completely as she sat down beside him and gently patted his hand. 'Strong, sweet tea is said to work
wonders——'

'I can't stand sweet tea,' he snapped, impatiently
dragging free his hand. 'I don't feel in the least like
tea, I...oh, hell!' he groaned, his entire body tensing
in protest as his head dropped once again to her
shoulder.

'Patrick, will you stop being so damned macho, for
heaven's sake?' she protested softly. 'Fred and José
are your friends and you love them...what's so terrible about shedding a few tears of relief on their
behalf?'

'Nothing—everything! Since that last day in
Gamborra, I've felt as though...hell, at times it's as

though my reason's gone walkabout...I ...it's pointless trying to explain.'

'No, it isn't,' she told him firmly, slipping her arms round his shoulders and running her fingers gently, coaxingly through his hair. 'It was on that last day in Gamborra that I began feeling an almost kindred sympathy for poor old Alice in Wonderland...It's a feeling I've never really been able to shake off.'

'And I couldn't have helped matters for you any more than the Mad Hatter did for Alice!' he exclaimed morosely.

'That's ridiculous,' she chided, tugging in exasperation at his hair. 'Heaven only knows what might have become of me but for you!'

He gave a bellow of protest. 'God, but you're a sadistic bully, Carlisle,' he complained, his fingers becoming entangled with hers as they rubbed gingerly at his head. 'You're determined to have me in tears, come what may!'

He lifted his head, his eyes widening in sudden shock as they met hers. 'I shouldn't have woken you!' he exclaimed hoarsely, his gaze mesmerising.

'You didn't wake me,' she countered breathlessly, longing springing to urgent life and rampaging recklessly within her as their locked eyes exchanged their own blatant, wordless messages.

'OK, so I didn't wake you,' he muttered distractedly, drawing their entwined fingers from his head and pressing her hand against his cheek. 'But I shouldn't be——' He broke off, removing her hand from his face as though only then aware of his action. 'I suppose it's too late for me to start suggesting you wear a placard round your neck reading "do not touch",' he sighed with a wry smile.

'Do you think it would make any difference, even if we were both to wear one?' she responded incautiously, a tingling, shivering awareness pervading, her entire body as she equally incautiously linked her arms round his neck.

'Sophie, are you by any chance propositioning me?' he demanded with a soft, throaty chuckle.

She leaned back in the circle of the arms suddenly enfolding her, a sultry softness in her eyes as they wallowed in the explicit candour of the message in his.

'I think I——' The words froze on her lips, silenced by the brutal swiftness with which realisation began bombarding her. 'What on earth am I saying?' she groaned, dragging her arms from him and burying her face in her hands. 'There was a moment this morning when I found it almost impossible to accept the thoughtless irresponsibility with which I'd behaved... yet now... for one terrible moment I was on the verge of behaving in exactly the same way again!'

'You might have been—but I wasn't,' he told her quietly, releasing her. 'My problem last night wasn't a lack of contraceptives—it was losing my head to the extent of not even thinking about the subject, let alone taking precautions. And though I have to admit I seem to be in constant danger of losing my head over you, last night's irresponsibility is something I shall never be guilty of a second time... that I promise you.'

'Oh,' was all she could manage, as his words finally sank in, before pausing for several seconds to await the outcome of the decidedly one-sided battle suddenly being fought within her. Then she straightened, adding with sudden firmness. 'And yes, I was—propositioning you.'

For an instant he gave her a look unabashed incredulity, then fell back across the bed, laughter rumbling weakly from him.

'You're not supposed to laugh!' she complained indignantly, scrabbling to her knees beside him.

'I know, but...' His words immediately deteriorated into another bout of helpless laughter.

Almost speechless with wounded pride, she grabbed him by the shoulders and attempted to shake him. 'What's happened to this constant danger you're supposed to be in of losing your head over me?' she demanded furiously, abandoning her unsuccessful attempts to shake him and grabbing him by the hair instead.

'I am, I am,' he groaned through his laughter, sliding his arms around her. 'But stop pulling my hair! I've a nasty feeling you'll beat me to a pulp if I complain of a headache,' he added with a throaty chuckle, 'particularly after having propositioned me so blatantly.'

He drew her head down to his, silencing her indignant protests with the urgent probings of his mouth on hers, a tremor of impatience in his hands as they swiftly removed the nightgown from her trembling, yielding body.

'I thought I'd propositioned you rather subtly,' she informed him with prim breathlessness while methodically undoing his shirt buttons before yanking it free from his trousers. 'You're not exactly co-operative,' she complained when he made not the slightest move to assist her with the removal of his shirt.

'I was waiting until you'd undone the cuffs—or had you forgotten about those?' he murmured innocently—an innocence wickedly contradicted by the sultry darkness of desire smouldering in the eyes following her every movement.

Then he was impatiently shrugging free of his shirt, pulling her down into his arms.

'Sophie, why don't you just come out with it and tell me what a monumental fool I am?' he groaned, his mouth searching hungrily for hers.

'You're a monumental fool,' she managed, despite the impassioned onslaught of his mouth on hers.

'I know I am,' he retorted, commencing to perform acrobatic feats that had her chuckling with unabashed pleasure and amazement as he discarded the remainder of his clothing. 'And that's ninety-nine per cent of the cure,' he continued, clasping her meltingly eager body to his.

'What is?' she gasped distractedly, shaken by the ferocity of longing with which her body was responding to the flagrant message of his.

'Knowing and admitting what a fool I am,' he murmured huskily, his enthusiastically exploring hands bringing soft, sighing cries from her with their restless, sensuous search. 'Admitting that your attitude is far wiser than mine; knowing that I should take a leaf out of your book and accept the way things are . . . the way I feel about you. Because that's what you've done, isn't it, my beautiful, very wise Sophie?'

'It wasn't wisdom—I had no option,' she choked, thoroughly distracted by the increasingly blatant messages his hands and body were now spelling out.

'And neither had I,' he groaned. 'Today I was little better than a sleep-walker . . . lost in dreams of your magic . . . of holding you like this again.' Then his lips and body were like a fire consuming hers, demanding and promising as her hands began following the impatient lead of his and his name became a chanted mantra of love on her lips.

'Love me,' she cried out, unable to hold back the words as her body goaded his with a tempestuous wantonness, unconditionally offering the love she had so carelessly begged from him.

And the unbridled passion with which he answered her cry filled her once more with that reckless, irrational joy that promised her she was truly loved. Even as the wildness of his passion met equal match in hers, sweeping through her in wave after wave of boundless rapture, there was that positive joy in her— banishing all possibility of doubt. And when his body drove hers beyond the confines of reason, to a timeless moment of exquisite fulfilment, the sobs that sighed from her were still a product of that same illusory joy.

'Sophie . . . you aren't crying, are you?' he demanded hesitantly, holding her tightly to him as he drew the quilt over them.

'Of course I'm not . . . at least, I don't think I am,' she finished uncertainly, burying her face against the curving warmth of his neck as that treacherous joy began wavering, then slowly drifting from her.

'You . . . you haven't any regrets?'

'No . . . and you?'

'Not so much as a ghost of one . . . except, perhaps, that I didn't face up to reality right from the start,' he whispered huskily, the tenderness in his words, seductive in their hint of promise, tearing gaping holes in the resolution she was desperately making never again to allow her own wishful fantasies to overwhelm her with such totality.

'Sophie, I can't change the way I am—I'd be an even greater fool than I already am to pretend I could,' he continued quietly. 'We seem to have started off where some lovers end up... perhaps time will give us the chance to unravel all that ... to work things out for ourselves.'

Confused and uncertain whether those words offered hope or had snatched it completely away, and with her confusion only compounded by the tenderness of the lingering kiss he then placed on her parted lips, she took the only option open to her and snuggled into his arms and into the thought-free escape of sleep.

CHAPTER NINE

'PATRICK, stop waffling on about arranging a passport for me,' begged Sophie, laughing. 'You've a load of far more important things to see to before catching that plane tonight.'

'I don't want you stranded here on your own,' he insisted stubbornly. 'You never know, it could be a couple of weeks or more before I'm back. And anyway, Rick Mason at the British Embassy has said he'll——'

'Get me a replacement passport as soon as humanly possible,' Sophie finished with gentle exasperation. 'So stop worrying.'

'Hell, I must remember to get our marriage certificate round to him!'

'Patrick!' she wailed, abandoning the dishwasher she had been emptying to watch with affectionate disbelief as he began furiously searching through the jumble of papers heaped on the kitchen table before him. She sneaked up behind him and hugged him tightly.

'Keep your hands to yourself, Carlisle,' he growled menacingly, reaching back to ruffle her hair. 'You know I'm putty in them—and, you're right, I've a load of things I have to see to before leaving tonight.'

A soft smile of contentment played round Sophie's lips as he gave an exaggerated sigh and began jotting down notes on the pad at his elbow. It had been a day as close to perfection as she had ever experienced, beginning with his bringing her breakfast in bed—chocolate and *churros* which he bare-facedly claimed to have concocted himself and for which he had obviously sent out—and developing with gentle, bantering tenderness despite the disruptive consequences of the telephone call that had come within an hour of her wakening.

'That was Valery Turyanov,' he had told her. 'The Russians have it from an impeccable source inside Gamborra that rebel morale is deteriorating at a rate of knots and that their surveys are dashing all their greedy hopes of unlimited treasures.'

Sophie had been jubilant. 'Thank heavens for that! What do you think will happen now?'

'With a bit of luck, they could well slink out just as quietly as they slunk in . . . it would give me a great deal of satisfaction to be there to record their exodus,' he had told her, igniting a now familiar tingling excitement in her by slipping an arm around her and lightly brushing her lips with his. 'That was from Valery—sort of—he sent his regards . . . and this is exclusively from me,' he had added, taking her fully into his arms and kissing her with an uninhibitedly hot-blooded enthusiasm. He had sworn with an almost equal lack of inhibition when the phone had again rung, tearing himself from her with voluble reluctance.

That second call had been from Fred and José, confirming Valery's information and echoing Patrick's eagerness to be on the spot when the end finally came.

'They want me to join them in Zambia as soon as I possibly can, so that ours is the team sitting on the doorstep ready for when those rats start deserting,' he had said, thereafter launching into frenetic action.

'You're going to need money!' he exclaimed suddenly, dragging her out of her thoughts. 'I'll leave you plenty of cash—and I can sign some cheques for——'

'Patrick, please!' she protested, aware there were far more pressing things to which he should attend, but secretly hugging herself with delight at his obvious preoccupation with her welfare. 'Go and do all those things you have to do! There's that equipment José wants—you'll have to get cracking for them to get it together in time to be on your flight. And there's your packing—if I knew what you need and where it is——'

'Can't wait to see the back of me,' he teased, leaping to his feet and swinging her into his arms.

She clung to him, the realisation that within hours she would be without him only now sinking fully in and filling her with an almost panicking desperation. 'Patrick, I——' She bit back her words of love—but only just.

'Oh, Sophie,' he groaned softly. 'If only...' He shook his head, then drew her firmly from him. 'Unfortunately, you're right—I'm cutting things far too fine.' His expression was one of wry regret as he bent down and placed a kiss on the tip of her nose. 'I'm afraid that by the time I'm through it'll be a case of tearing back here, throwing a few things together and piling myself into a cab.'

'I wish there were more I could do,' whispered Sophie, her words lost to him as he released her, grabbed several papers from the table and dashed out. 'I suppose I could make some coffee for the decorators,' she muttered to herself, gazing disconsolately around as she filled the kettle and realising how unbearably lonely and empty this huge apartment was going to seem without him . . . how unbearably lonely and empty life was going to be without him.

When seconds later he popped his head round the door and blew her a kiss before disappearing to the accompaniment of the heavy slam of the front door, she abandoned the kettle and sped to the drawing-room. Dismissing the small inner voice accusing her of behaving like a besotted child, she waited by one of the windows, feeling the ruched silk of the curtains heavy against her shoulder as she watched for his familiar figure to appear on the street below.

Despite the brightness of the sun there was a sharp, almost cool edge to the quality of the light, which reminded her of something she had once read about painters regarding the light in Madrid as uniquely special. She felt she almost understood what those painters had meant as a young woman strolled into her line of vision, her vivid, dark-haired beauty creating a stunning picture of its own before she disappeared into the building.

She found herself wondering idly if the girl lived in the block, then how many apartments it contained. She had just got round to wondering where on earth Patrick had got to, when he appeared. The stunning young woman was by his side—the top of her head barely reaching his shoulder, a point brought very much home to Sophie in her state of virtual trance when Patrick slipped an arm round his companion and drew her close to his side, his gesture all but concealing the girl's head from sight.

She saw no more. Her next conscious awareness was of being back in the kitchen, sitting at the table and struggling to replenish the breath that seemed to have been squeezed in its entirety from her starved lungs.

She had been through all this one way or another before, protested a small, sane voice within her. Whether or not that had been Anna altered nothing. If she were to bump into Steven, would they not greet one another rapturously—would he think twice about slipping an arm around her as they walked along?

She rose and went to the utility-room off the kitchen and began sorting through a basket of clothes to be ironed. Patrick had told her to leave them, that the housekeeper would be back to attend to such things once the bulk of the decorators' work was finished. Now she tackled the task she so loathed as though fulfilling a craving.

It was only when the sick tension gripping her finally began to ease that she was even aware of the strength of its hold on her. And it was crazy of her to have reacted like that, she scolded herself, it just wasn't like her. There was no way Patrick could be described as another Robert, albeit an unmarried one. Unlike Robert, the only words of love Patrick would ever speak would be tantamount to a vow, hence his understandable caution. For heaven's sake, he had had his arm round a woman-friend and there had been nothing in the least furtive in his action!

She gathered together the ironing, pulling a small face at the sight of the pile she had got through . . . it served her damn well right for reacting so idiotically!

The sudden chime of the doorbell brought a frown of puzzlement to her brow, then she put down the pile of ironing in her arms and raced out into the hall.

Close up, the woman standing at the door looked even more delicately beautiful than she had from the

street below. Probably a couple of years older than
Sophie, she was a good few inches shorter, though
her blue-black hair, piled high in careless profusion
on top of her head, added a little to her height. The
heavily lashed eyes that gazed with such confidence
into Sophie's seemed to glow with the rich warmth of
amber.

All in all, this vision of perfection was one of the
most beautiful women Sophie had ever seen.

Coolly the woman reached out a hand. 'I am Anna
Contesti y Carreras.'

'I'm afraid Patrick isn't here,' said Sophie, the first
words to enter her head and completely unnecessary
ones, given that this woman probably knew Patrick's
movements far better than she.

'I know,' smiled Anna, sweeping serenely in past
her. 'The poor darling is tearing all over the place.'
She slipped off her elegant silk jacket, draping it non-
chalantly over a huge ornamental vase in the hall
before proceeding, with the air of one completely at
home, to the kitchen. 'With Patrick it's always a hectic
dash before he sets off on an assignment, but today
I've had enough and abandoned him. I decided it
would be far more pleasant to come here and have
coffee with you instead of being dragged all over the
place by him.'

Sophie was just about to respond to that blatant
hint when her impromptu visitor set about preparing
the coffee herself.

'Well, you obviously know where everything is,'
Sophie observed, a shade tartly, then sat down, seeds
of animosity taking firm root in her as a lilting peal
of laughter assaulted her ears.

'I should hope I know where everything is; this is, after all, more or less my second home.' She switched on the percolator, turning her attention on Sophie with a small exclamation. 'I'm so silly, I keep forgetting that you and Patrick are virtual strangers!' she exclaimed. 'He obviously wouldn't feel any need to tell you about me.'

'Obviously,' agreed Sophie, outwardly calm, while inwardly churning with uncertainty and a totally irrational feeling of foreboding. Then she was racking her brains for something to say as the silence between them grew markedly heavier. Yet the more frantically she searched, the less able she became to find a single pertinent word. 'My name's Sophie,' she announced in desperation, adding tensely, 'though you probably already know that.'

'Yes...it's a lovely name,' responded Anna expressionlessly, then joined her at the table.

It was the unmistakable tremor in the hand with which the Spanish girl passed her a cup that changed the entire atmosphere between them, giving Sophie a sudden and startled insight into feelings every bit as tense and uncertain as her own beneath the abrasive coolness of that self-confident exterior.

'It was wrong of me to come,' blurted out Anna, the vulnerable diffidence now in her eyes extinguishing every last spark of Sophie's irrational feelings of animosity. 'I was so confused and upset until Patrick explained to me about the marriage...but I still can't quite shake off those terrible feelings. I'm used to reading rumours about him in the British Press...but to read that the man you are to marry has suddenly married someone else——' She broke off with a helpless shrug.

Sophie froze; parts of her—vitally essential parts—ceasing to function. She picked up her cup and drained it of its scalding contents, welcoming the physical pain as a distraction from the remaining parts of her still functioning which urgently warned her she was about to be violently sick.

'You must think me terribly stupid!' exclaimed the Spanish girl. 'But I——'

'No,' croaked Sophie, striving for control over her wildly careering emotions. 'No... of course I don't think that,' she managed, slightly startled to find she was still actually capable of speech. 'But surely you realise that once this marriage is ended it will be as though it had never happened.' she heard herself continue, and immediately wondered where she had found the words, let alone the ability to utter them.

'That's what Patrick keeps telling me,' said Anna, her eyes oddly watchful as they met Sophie's.

'Yes... I'm sure he does,' muttered Sophie, conscious that shock alone constituted the fragile barrier between her mind and the tidal wave of reaction about to engulf her. 'And you must realise that, if it hadn't been for Patrick's exceptional kindness, I dread to think what might have happened to me.' A fact she must keep in mind at all costs, she warned herself frantically as she felt her flimsy defences falter and start to crumble.

'The papers all said how beautiful you are,' sighed Anna wistfully, as though lost in her own private thoughts. 'And you *are*... so very beautiful.'

'It's very sweet of you to say so,' managed Sophie, as mental hell began breaking loose in her. How could she have let herself be so utterly deceived? How could he have done this to her? Today, which only moments

before had seemed close to perfection, had been re-
duced to nothing more than an empty sham.

Her mind leapt suddenly into violent overdrive—
dredging up every word Patrick had ever uttered regarding the way things might be once the marriage
was behind them. No wonder he had offered her no
more than those vague, guarded hints—he had been
too pious for honest-to-goodness lies! And no wonder,
either, that he claimed to hold such strong views on
the sanctity of marriage, having already chosen the
woman who would one day be his wife!

She rose to her feet, stalling for time to collect her
rampaging thoughts by painstakingly slowly helping
herself to more coffee. All it had taken was those few
enlightening words from the silent girl at the table for
everything to fall so sickeningly into perspective, she
realised with a savage, burning bitterness. He loved
and would one day marry Anna, but until that day
came he obviously had few qualms about allowing
the powerful sexual attraction he felt towards another
woman to take its inevitable course. Perhaps because
he sensed her desperate need of them he had felt
obliged to mouth those elusive half-promises, those
equivocal references to a future once they were free.
She had judged him to be a man of integrity, yet all
he had been was a ruthless schemer whose highly
selective conscience would have preferred it had their
temporary marriage been neatly over and done with.
And how dreadfully inconvenient he had found it
when the chemistry between them had proved more
powerful than even his practised scheming could
handle!

'I shall be out of both your lives very soon now,'
she declared decisively, returning to the table. 'Now

that Fred and José are free there's no need for the pretence to be kept up any longer.'

It would serve the lying, sanctimonious hypocrite right if she *was* pregnant, she told herself, her silent rage deepening as she remembered his reactions to that possibility. He had claimed to consider life too short to worry over a problem that might never exist—how pat his claims seemed now. He had spoken of guilt, but how quickly he had bounced back to normal, with no sign of guilt to dampen his ardour once he had given vent to his pride's resentment at having so completely lost control of his passions. Why couldn't he have been honest? Because he wanted to have his cake and to eat it, she replied to her own impassioned question with ruthless candour, something she earnestly prayed honesty would have denied him.

'I'll be leaving Spain the moment my passport is ready,' she promised—a promise made to herself. 'And the—ending of the marriage should be no more than a formality once the true story is out.'

There was an almost childlike quality to Anna's smile. 'I know I'm wrong to get so jealous, but sometimes it's difficult loving a man like Patrick.'

With considerable difficulty, Sophie forced an answering smile to her lips, the spontaneous flash of jealousy searing through her at those innocent words a harsh reminder of the love burning on within her despite the vehemence of her hatred. 'I ... I'm sure I'd have had similar feelings ... had it happened to me. But now that Patrick has explained, surely you must see that you had absolutely nothing to worry about,' she said, doggedly ignoring the din of protest shrieking out within her as she strove to reassure the girl.

'Yes...I do know that,' whispered Anna, her vulnerable hesitancy a very far cry from her almost aggressive self-confidence of scarcely minutes before. 'And I feel guilty for having come here...I just felt I had to see you for myself.'

'I understand,' replied Sophie gently. 'And I don't really see that there's any need to tell Patrick of this visit, do you?'

Anna shook her head, her face suddenly curiously expressionless as she dropped her eyes from Sophie's.

She really was quite outstandingly beautiful, thought Sophie, though the pangs of jealousy accompanying that thought were strongly tempered by a sharp stab of pity for this girl whom she knew to have been so grossly deceived. Then her pity too was being dissipated in the sudden flash of memory of all Patrick's good points—and despite his callous treachery, he had many... Once married to Anna, his commitment would be total and he would never deliberately cause her any hurt.

'I really ought to be going,' announced the Spanish girl, rising.

'I'll see you out,' offered Sophie, dread filling her at the prospect of being alone with the devastation of her thoughts.

'You've been so kind—so understanding,' sighed Anna, as they stepped into the sunshine. For an instant she paused, then took a breath as though she was about to add something. But she said nothing, instead she leaned over and lightly brushed each of Sophie's cheeks with her own.

Kindness and understanding couldn't have been further from her present feelings, thought Sophie grimly as she watched Anna get into an expensive sports car and drive off. She had been living in a fool's paradise even thinking he could ever love her, when all the time his love—if not his faithfulness—had been Anna's.

She turned and made her way slowly back into the building, tensed in anticipation of the horrors of the devastation about to hit her, yet experiencing no more than a curiously light-headed detachment. She hesitated as she reached the foot of the staircase in the cool marbled foyer, then walked on past it and out into the central courtyard.

She sat down on one of the sun-warmed benches, oblivious of the lush, colour-splashed serenity of her surroundings as her mind began systematically searching out, sorting and replaying every relevant memory stored within it. With a ruthless detachment hitherto alien to her, she examined and re-examined every nuance of every word—of every look, even— that had passed between them, till she finally lifted her face towards the now sinking sun and closed her eyes.

How willing a victim she had been, yet how calculating and totally unprincipled had been his deception. And it was his lack of principles to which he had so sanctimoniously laid claim that made his behaviour so utterly despicable.

Later she heard the workmen leave and felt a small stab of guilt . . . it now seemed a lifetime ago since she had started to fill the kettle to make them coffee.

She rose and reluctantly made her way back to the apartment. She would confront him with his despicable hypocrisy, she vowed, her detachment now giving way to an anger fuelled by a terrible sense of humiliation. But she was shaking her head as she entered the bathroom and began running a bath. No...she couldn't confront him. There was her promise to Anna not to mention her visit...and then there was what remained of her pride.

Slowly, she began undressing. What precious little he had left her of her pride was the only thing holding her together, she reminded herself harshly...but, however little it was, it was all she had left to hang on to.

'Sophie, I'm back! Where are you?'

'I'm having a bath,' she called out, the lie tripping from her with ease as she stood in the bathroom, long since bathed and dressed.

'I'm afraid I'll have to ring for a cab right now—I've cut it rather fine.'

She knew precisely how fine he had cut it, having consulted her watch probably as many times in the past thirty minutes. But she also knew she couldn't face him. Just the sound of his voice, just the knowledge of his presence and all her reserve was starting to crumble.

Frantically she grabbed a towel and buried her face in it. What resolve? The anger—the detachment—everything that had kept her going from almost the instant of Anna's shattering disclosure had now deserted her...now there was only the unbearable hurt...the devastating sense of loss.

She buried her face deeper into the towel as she heard him rap lightly on the door, praying for the strength to overcome the pain now rising to a sobbing crescendo within her.

'I've got you some money and I've signed a few cheques for you. Rick's dealing with your passport and he'll ring you in a few days. Sophie, why are you using this bathroom?'

She took a deep, shuddering breath. 'I thought you might want to use yours.'

'May I come in?'

'No!' She took another, even deeper breath. 'I'll be out in a moment—you'd better get your things together.'

In her mind's eye she could see the the expression of puzzlement on his handsome features as she was aware of his hesitation before he spoke again.

'Yes, I suppose I'd better...the cab will be here in a few minutes.'

A few minutes, she repeated numbly to herself. And she owed it to herself to survive these last few minutes—once they were behind her she would be free to blot him from her mind and from her life forever.

He was in the kitchen when she entered it, the impact of his presence catching her unawares like a sudden and violent blow in the stomach as he looked up from the familiar leather duffel bag open before him on the table.

The slightly diffident smile with which he greeted her was like a further bombardment of blows. 'Darling, I told you not to bother with the ironing— that someone would be in to do it,' he chided, throwing a couple of the shirts she had earlier ironed into the bag, then closing it.

It was his casual use of that term of endearment— something that earlier would only have served as ballast to her foolish illusions—that overrode the ache of longing the sight of him had aroused in her.

'There's nothing like a spot of something as boring as ironing to help concentrate the mind—and I had some serious thinking to do.' She felt sure there was nothing in her tone to alert him, a feeling that brought her a certain bitter pride, and it threw her when she sensed an immediate and almost imperceptible tensing in him.

'And the outcome of all this serious thinking?' he asked, his tone devoid of expression though his eyes had narrowed watchfully.

'Just that I managed to put one or two things back into their correct perspective,' she stated woodenly, nervously ramming her hands into the pockets of her jeans as she felt them clench in agitation. She had walked into this room with no clear thought in her head save to survive the next few minutes . . . an act of sheer lunacy, given that they had parted as lovers . . .

'Sophie, you obviously have something on your mind—so out with it, the cab will be here any minute.'

'Honesty!' The word seemed to explode from her like an expletive and she immediately found herself scrabbling around for others to detract from its rash impetuousness—the last thing she could risk was to confront him. 'What I meant was——'

'That you feel I haven't been completely honest with you? Sophie, this is hardly the time to be bringing up a subject like that.'

The utter deviousness of those almost impatient words took her breath away. She had considered Robert the lowest of the low for his lies—but this sanctimonious hypocrite couldn't even bring himself to lie by denying he had been dishonest with her!

'The honesty—or lack of it—concerning me was my own,' she lied almost with relish, her thoughts suddenly honing in on a blurred image of Robert. 'I wasn't honest about my reasons for being in

Gamborra... my father didn't approve of the man I was in love with—that's why I left England.'

'A story which sounds remarkably similar to the one you and I concocted for the militia,' he stated coldly.

'Yes—I suppose I automatically suggested a variation on the truth,' she muttered, racking her brains in an attempt to remember which of them had actually come up with that embellishment—not that it mattered now she had claimed it as hers.

'And why do you feel this sudden urge to confide in me—now of all times?'

'Because...' Her eyes rose unflinchingly to the chill scrutiny of his. 'Because I still love him... I'm going back to him.'

'Just let me get this straight,' he intoned softly, his eyes cold slits of disbelief. 'You love a man, yet you shed your virginity to another—a virtual stranger?'

Not a virtual stranger, she cried out silently, but a complete and utter stranger... not that she would ever have believed it at the time. 'People who end up in bed together aren't necessarily in love,' she retorted coldly. '*You* should know that!'

'Oh, I know that, all right,' he stated venomously. 'But what I can't understand is how you didn't end up in bed with the man you claim to love.' He appeared not to have heard the sudden chime of the doorbell. 'And what intrigues me even more is your statement that you're going back to him. Are you sure he'll want you—now you've had your roll in the hay with me?'

'You really believe in calling a spade a spade, don't you, Patrick?' she lashed out savagely, hurt beyond measure by the flippant dismissiveness of his words. 'Robert won't mind . . . he loves me!'

He picked up his bag and slung it over one shoulder as the bell rang again, then he strode to her side. 'I suggest you forget any idea you have of hot-footing it back to lover boy for the time being.' He grabbed her firmly by the shoulder as she made to escape him. 'And as for calling a spade a spade—I think the time has come to start calling it a shovel,' he told her with chilling softness. 'No man—not even if he's a paragon who worships the ground you walk on—will ever be given the option of playing father to any child of mine. Is that plain enough for you?'

'You're mad!' she protested, struggling to break free. 'The chances of my being pregnant are very slight!'

'But they exist,' he drawled coldly, releasing her. 'I shan't be here to stop you doing whatever you choose, but the fact is you're married to me . . . and I have no intention of starting divorce proceedings until I have valid medical proof that you're not pregnant.'

He turned and marched out of the room.

'Patrick! What do you mean—valid medical proof?' she cried, racing out after him. 'You don't honestly believe I'd lie to you over something like that?'

He opened the front door, then turned, his face pale with rage. 'Sophie, right now I wouldn't trust you to give me an honest reply were I to ask you the time . . . does that answer your question?'

CHAPTER TEN

'AND that's it?' exclaimed Dorothy Shaba, horrified. 'You got your passport, came back to England and neither saw nor heard from him until yesterday's phone call?'

'Yes...I mean, no...he tracked me down at my parents' place in Henfield,' muttered Sophie agitatedly, part of her almost regretting the complete frankness with which she had confided in her friend as the vicious pain from her freshly opened wounds began dulling her mind.

'What—he went there?'

'No...he rang.'

'And?'

'I repeated what I'd told him in the note I left for him in Madrid—that I wasn't pregnant. And I said I wanted out of the marriage the quickest way legalities permitted.'

'And how did he react?' quizzed Dorothy.

'He reminded me of the medical certificate he'd asked for, confirming I wasn't pregnant, then he told me that he couldn't start any action anyway as he was off on an assignment to India.'

'Yes...I remember seeing something of his on India not so long ago,' said Dorothy, then she gave a sigh. 'Sophie, this is all too ghastly for words...you know, you really should have had the whole thing out with him in Madrid.'

'That's easy to say now,' whispered Sophie, her face tense and pale. 'But then...the thought of making an even bigger fool of myself than he'd already done——' She broke off with a helpless shrug.

'It strikes me that he doesn't exactly seem to have been in a frantic rush to end this marriage of yours,' remarked Dorothy quietly.

'I've already explained this odd fixation he has that I might be pregnant, and besides, he's hardly had the time,' pointed out Sophie wearily. 'They were in Gamborra for several weeks; first of all covering the return of the deposed government, then doing that documentary on Gamborran life in the aftermath of the coup.'

'On Gamborran life—yes,' agreed Dorothy. 'It was one of the best documentaries I've ever seen . . . but there was hardly what you'd describe as any aftermath to that ridiculous coup—the people just got on with their lives as they always had.' There was a glint of exasperation in the gentle brown of her eyes as they met those of her friend. 'Sophie, love, what on earth possessed you to bury yourself down in Sussex like that for all those weeks?' she chided gently.

'I told you, I had a bad dose of flu,' whispered Sophie, her pale cheeks colouring. So many times she had begun dialling Dorothy's number—always stopping before ever completing it until yesterday. 'It's taken me an age to get over it.'

'But not this long,' stated Dorothy with forthright candour. 'Sophie, the last thing you needed was to be alone with all that heartache bottled up inside you,' she sighed. 'And you know that all you needed to do was pick up a phone and either Susie or I would have dropped everything and come running——' She broke off, pulling a small face. 'On second thoughts, perhaps Susie wouldn't have been such a good bet.'

'You mean her idiotic crush on Patrick?' murmured Sophie, wan amusement softening her drawn features.

'Precisely,' agreed the Gamborran girl wryly. 'I've never understood how such an otherwise highly intelligent person could have so juvenile a crush on a total stranger—no matter how gorgeous . . . oh, hell!' she groaned. 'Me and my big mouth!'

'He's gorgeous all right,' agreed Sophie as her embarrassed friend hastily began inspecting the contents of the teapot.

'I think this has had it—shall I make some more?' she asked diffidently.

'Dorothy, I'm not about to have the vapours just because you mentioned his name,' Sophie protested gently. 'And don't make more tea for me—I'm fine.'

'If only you *were* fine,' sighed the Gamborran girl, gazing up anxiously at her. 'Sophie, would you mind if I indulged in a bit of delving?' she asked suddenly.

'Delving?' echoed Sophie cautiously. 'I suppose not,' she muttered, then added more positively, 'Why not? You're right, Dorothy, it's been a nightmare having all this bottled up inside me. It would be dishonest not to admit it hurts like mad talking about it . . . but I can already feel some of those ghastly knots inside me loosening up.' Except that they would tighten up once more with a vengeance the instant she left this sanctuary . . . the instant she left to meet Patrick once again.

'Good . . . it's just that I've a feeling you've been in such a state you might not be seeing the wood for the trees. For instance, the possibility doesn't even seem to have occurred to you that, despite the girlfriend, this guy could well have fallen in love with you.'

Sophie shook her head in violent protest. 'Of course he didn't! He would have told me . . . explained.'

'And how many times did you tell him you loved him?' countered Dorothy quietly.

'That's not fair,' protested Sophie hoarsely. 'And you're forgetting that I saw him with her. A man just doesn't behave towards a woman he no longer loves the way he did to her.'

'I'm sorry, love,' sighed Dorothy, rising and seating herself on the arm of Sophie's chair. 'It was just a thought . . . and from much of what you've described of him, he doesn't really sound like your average sort of rat.' She placed an arm round Sophie and gave her a hug. 'I hate seeing you like this. And I also hate feeling so completely useless! Would it help if I came along with you?'

Sophie gave the girl's hand a reassuring squeeze as she shook her head. 'No, it's sweet of you to offer, but this is something I have to face alone. I'm hoping that all it will entail is the signing of a few forms . . . then it will be over.'

'What—you're meeting at his solicitor's office?' demanded Dorothy, surprised.

Sophie shook her head, a look of hopelessness on her face as her gaze dropped. 'Dorothy, one thing I haven't done is get that doctor's letter he asked for,' she whispered hoarsely.

'Did he bring it up again yesterday?'

Sophie shook her head. 'But that doesn't guarantee he won't today,' she sighed.

'Only a complete and utter fruit cake would insist on something like that!' exclaimed Dorothy exasperatedly. 'Are you completely sure you don't want me to come?'

'No, I'll be all right, I promise. All I want now is to have whatever it is I have to face over and behind me...as quickly as possible.' Her heart started up a heavy, painful thudding as she glanced down at her watch. 'And I really ought to be on my way now,' she added, rising.

'Relax, love, I'll run you there,' murmured Dorothy, her alert, anxious eyes missing nothing. 'And there's really no need I can see for you to go haring back to Sussex afterwards—are you sure you won't spend the night?'

Sophie hesitated, finding her mind incapable of looking beyond the prospect of what lay immediately ahead of her.

'Don't decide now. See how you feel later and give me a ring,' suggested Dorothy. 'And just keep it in mind that though friends are great to have around in the good times...it's in the bad times that they can really prove their worth.'

And she needed a friend right now, fretted Sophie, deliberately slowing her steps as she climbed the stairs to Patrick's flat. Someone to help her through this time far worse than bad.

Her steps slowed further as she attempted to bring some order to the chaotic churning and knotting within her that was turning her breathing into an almost laboured pant.

It was six weeks—practically to the day—since she had last seen him, yet the empty despair, the raging hurt, the numbing sense of devastation were as fresh and acute now as they had been that day six weeks ago in Madrid.

'Sophie?'

She glanced up, freezing at the familiar sound of that softly lilting voice. She needed more time, she protested frantically—time in which to gain a shred of composure...time in which to turn and run.

He was dragging a heavy navy sweater over his head as she reached the open doorway in which he stood.

'Come in—it's cold,' he muttered, turning from her.

'Yes.' She followed him through, her eyes feasting with an insatiable hunger on his tall, lean figure.

He was in dire need of a haircut, she thought, startled that so mundane a thought should have formed in the jumbled chaos of her mind.

'I've coffee on—would you like some?'

She nodded. He looked tired, and unusually pale beneath his tan, she thought, this man whose image had occupied her every waking moment for what now seemed a lifetime...this man she still loved despite everything, yet hardly knew.

She followed him into the living-room.

'I'll take your coat,' he offered, in tones she had difficulty interpreting...she recognised its surface coolness; what lay beneath was beyond her.

She hesitated slightly before removing her coat and handing it to him. This was far worse than even her most nightmarish imaginings, she thought, a shiver of apprehension rippling through her as she watched him leave the room. Once their bodies had entwined in a passion so sweetly overwhelming there was no dream that could ever equal it...now she was having difficulty merely gauging what lay beneath the rigid mask of his cold social platitudes.

She sat down on the sofa, unnerved by the path her thoughts were taking.

'Are your eyes completely better?' he asked, returning with two mugs and handing her one.

'Yes, thank you.' She took a sip, every nerve in her straining to snapping-point. She should never have taken off her coat—never have accepted the coffee. If she had had any sense at all, she would have demanded that they conduct whatever business they had on the doorstep.

'Are you nursing again yet?'

'No...I ended up with a bad bout of flu after I got home...' As her words trailed to a halt, she felt something in her snap. 'Patrick, we both know I'm not here on a social visit, so let's stop trying to pretend I am!'

'Who's pretending?' he drawled coolly, throwing his large body on to an armchair to the right of her, hooking one long leg over the arm-rest as he watched her with almost open hostility. 'You look rough—are you quite sure you're not pregnant?'

'For God's sake, stop it!' she almost shrieked at him. 'Why do you have to keep on about that? I'm *not* pregnant! I've already told you I'm not!'

'Oh, yes—the note you left me in Madrid.'

'Yes!' she exclaimed sharply. Any moment now he would start demanding written proof, she thought bitterly. 'I *told* you I've had flu...and you're not exactly looking in peak form yourself!' Nice one, Sophie, she groaned furiously to herself. Incisive invective of that calibre would soon have his supercilious cool in shreds! She leaned forward and placed her mug on the table before her, battling to get a grip on herself. 'You asked me here about the divorce. Obviously it's in both our interests to get it settled as quickly as possible, so please, Patrick, could we get on with discussing it?' That was a lot better, she congratulated herself, doggedly ignoring the brittle tension now almost paralysing her.

'Perhaps India didn't agree with me,' he drawled, studiously ignoring her plea. 'The entire time I was there, I——'

'Patrick—the divorce!' she cut in raggedly. 'I don't want to sit here playing cat-and-mouse games with you.'

'Perhaps *I* do,' he responded with chilling softness, the cold glitter of granite in the eyes making their leisurely sweep of her tensely hunched figure. 'But there again, being a fairly good-natured sort, I'll try to resist the temptation,' he added in that same chilling tone. 'I'm sure you must be bursting to catch up on all my news since we last met—despite your professed eagerness to get straight to business.'

'Patrick . . . please,' choked Sophie. She was trembling from head to foot and knew without doubt that if she didn't get away from here soon—away from this coldly taunting stranger—she was in danger of snapping completely.

'You'll no doubt be pleased to hear I visited your nuns and gave them reassurances as to your state of health.'

'Thank you,' she blurted out, caught by the sheer unexpectedness of those words. 'It was very kind of you.'

'Yes, wasn't it?' he murmured silkily. 'Now, what about your news. How's what's-his-name—Robert, wasn't it?' His face darkened in sudden fury. 'Quite content to take another man's leavings, was he?' he exploded harshly, both the words and their stark ferocity making Sophie cringe with horror.

'Would you please get me my coat?' she managed through lips painfully parched. 'I want to go.' She *had* to go!

'But I haven't finished. I haven't yet told you about my little jaunt to India,' he murmured, his sudden switch back to silky softness filling her with a sickening sensation of unreality. 'Nor my eventual return to Madrid . . . and, of course, to Anna.'

Sophie rose to her feet, her face deathly pale.

'Sit down, Sophie,' he ordered quietly, his eyes suddenly wavering from the blaze of hers. 'Hell . . . I apologise unreservedly for that remark about your boyfriend . . . it was worse than despicable. But you *will* sit down and you *will* listen to what I have to say.'

'You're right, you are utterly despicable, and don't you think it's a bit late to start telling me all this now?' she flung at him in better accusation. 'Any man with a shred of decency in him would have told me long ago!'

'Why don't you sit down and damn well listen?' he hurled back at her. 'Then we'll see which of us should be dishing out the insults!'

She sat down, her action almost reflex, balancing stiffly on the very edge of the sofa as though still poised for flight.

'Once upon a time,' he began, a sneer twisting his face.

Sophie closed her eyes, suddenly very close to tears. She was beginning to understand exactly how a trapped animal must feel.

'Anna's mother and mine have been close friends since childhood,' he stated, his tone completely matter-of-fact as he again switched from one extreme to the other.

Sophie's eyes opened to find herself still the object of his ceaseless scrutiny. But the sneer was gone, and now his face was expressionless—a blank canvas yet to be filled.

'It became a standard joke between them—when we were still children—that Anna and I would eventually marry. It was something that had been bandied around for almost as long as I can remember, and something that she and I joined in and indulged our mothers with. But it was always a joke—perhaps there was a time when our mothers harboured secret hopes, but as no pressure was ever brought to bear on either of us I honestly doubt it.' He got to his feet and began pacing back and forth. 'My mother wasn't too happy with me before she left for Ireland—because I'd forgotten to let Anna know about my marriage to you. She considered it an appalling lack of manners on my part because Anna is regarded more or less as family.' He broke off his restless pacing to stand squarely before her. 'I've no idea what possessed her to visit you and tell you that ludicrous pack of lies about our impending marriage. Oh, yes, Anna came clean with me,' he told her harshly, as Sophie began mentally picking herself up from the floor. 'She was at her most melodramatic—beside herself at having discovered how desperately she loved me,' he added disparagingly. 'I should point out that Anna's more often than not beside herself with unrequited love—though, never before having been on the receiving end of it, I'd no idea quite how magnificent a performance she could give. It's what she thrives on most...it's a tragic waste she's not on the stage.'

Perhaps it was his derisive, almost jocular delivery that was giving her such problems, thought Sophie nervously...and she was having serious problems. She was hearing his words, understanding them without difficulty—yet there was this strange block inside her, its heavy, leaden dullness filling her, its stifling presence obstructing even her ability to react.

'Until yesterday, I regarded Anna with the grudging affection reserved for an irritating kid sister. Yesterday I found myself wanting to kill her... until I decided to come over here and kill you instead.'

Sophie gazed up at him blankly. Perhaps, had she been able to make any sense of those last words, she would have responded...because she could already sense the gradual disintegration of that inhibiting block within her as she felt herself respond to the scowling look of anger with which he gazed down on her.

'My God, can't you think of *anything* to say?' he exploded. 'Or are you suddenly deaf?'

'What do you expect me to say?' she cried out, leaping to her feet. 'I don't understand what you're saying! I've never really understood what you're saying! I can't think with you around!'

'Communication is my business,' he hurled at her savagely, grasping her by the arms. 'Thousands of people understand what I say...I'd be out of a job if they didn't. So why the hell should you have such problems?'

'I hate you!' she lashed out, childish in her fury.

'Do you, now?' he demanded harshly, his hands biting into her flesh. 'There was a time when I was almost convinced you loved me.'

'That only goes to show how easy it is to mistake infatuation for love,' she hurled at him in reckless outrage.

'You're right, because no woman who loved me would have even listened to Anna's drivel—let alone believed it! No one with even a smattering of understanding of me would have heeded her... yet you did, didn't you, Sophie?'

'Let go of me. Please... I can't think like this.'

'I'm beginning to wonder if you're capable of thought at all!' he exclaimed, shaking her in his exasperated impatience. 'Explain to me about Robert!' he demanded, once more careering off on a tangent that left her mind reeling.

'There's nothing to explain about Robert!' she bellowed as the dam within her broke, spilling out in a hot rush of tears. 'Robert was just an excuse... you're so stupid! I hate you, Patrick Carlisle, I hate you!' As her uncontrolled rush of words dried up on her, her exclusive thought was to spare herself the ultimate humiliation of his seeing the full extent of the state she was in. She buried her face in the only shelter available to her—the broad expanse of his chest.

'And I hate you too, Sophie Carlisle,' he groaned, his arms sliding possessively around her. 'As much as it's possible for a man to hate the woman he loves as I love you.'

'I don't understand how you can be so horrified at my believing Anna, when... what did you say?' she choked, every moving part of her jarring to a violent halt.

'God, but you're slow on the uptake, Carlisle!' he exclaimed, hugging her fiercely to him. 'I said that I love you. And if you open your mouth to tell me another lie, or to start hurling more abuse at me, I'll... oh, Sophie.' His lips moved against her cheek, hot and searching as they plundered the soft, tremulous welcome they found. 'Oh, Sophie, how I've missed you . . . how I've needed you,' he breathed raggedly against her mouth. 'How I've needed your presence, the sweet fire of your passion . . . but most of all, how I've needed your love . . . I need your love above all else!'

'And you have it—you know you have it,' she protested, as though in a dream. 'Lying to you was the only way I could hide how much I loved you.'

'Every instinct I possess told me you were lying,' he whispered passionately. 'But until I learned the tricks Anna had been up to, how could I possibly heed those instincts . . .? Sophie, I felt as though I was going out of my mind that night in Madrid . . . being out of my mind would have been sheer bliss compared to what I was going through!' He drew her down on to the sofa. 'Sophie, just tell me you love me,' he pleaded softly.

She turned towards him, placing her arms around his neck as love began bursting in sweet explosions of joy throughout her. 'I love you,' she whispered, unable to trust herself to say more.

His arms slid round her, cradling her in a fierce, almost suffocating hold against him. 'You have to realise, there aren't enough words around to describe how much I love you,' he whispered, his lips nuzzling softly against hers.

She had to struggle to free her arms, then she raised them up to cup his face in her hands. And as she gazed into the sultry green darkness of his eyes, she was trembling from the tumult of emotions hurtling through her. 'I've loved you for so long now, it seems like forever,' she choked, uncertain whether her sudden inability to breathe was being caused by the fierceness of his hold or the crazy welter of joy running amok throughout her. 'Couldn't you feel my love bombarding you . . . most of all when we made love?' she demanded huskily.

'Perhaps,' he murmured huskily. 'But then I could ask that same question of you.' He gave a soft groan of protest. 'You shouldn't have been in a position of having to detect whether or not I loved you!' he exclaimed distractedly. 'Sophie, I swear if it hadn't been for that wretched marriage I'd have had no hesitation in telling you how I felt . . . if you only knew how hard I found holding back those words when we made love.'

'You're talking to someone with a load of experience in that particular department,' she told him tremulously.

'Darling, I know I let the question of the marriage grow out of all proportion in my mind. But only because I felt I'd complicated the entire issue by falling in love with you——'

'Patrick, none of this matters any more,' she chided softly.

'Except that we still have to sort this marriage out.'

'By getting ourselves out of it,' she announced firmly. 'Because I never want you to feel trapped by loving me.'

'You what?' he exclaimed, drawing back from her clinging arms and gazing down at her in wide-eyed astonishment.

'Patrick, I know a lot of men feel uncertain about marriage—afraid, almost——'

'I don't.'

'And they feel that . . . I beg your pardon?'

'I said—I don't,' he repeated, an unreadable expression in his eyes as they held hers.

'Well, what I meant was...I mean, just because two people love one another, it doesn't mean to say they'd necessarily want to get married.'

'I take it you're speaking for yourself,' he said. 'Because, personally, I can't think of a better reason to get married—unless, of course, one of the parties happens to be in need of a passport.'

'Very funny,' she muttered uncertainly.

'Sophie, I've tried explaining what a serious commitment I regard marriage as. I've always made a hash of explaining why ours disturbed me quite as it did. It made me feel uncomfortable ultimately, because we'd entered into it for the wrong reasons, yet there I was loving you...it just didn't seem right. Can you understand that?' he demanded with sudden intensity.

She nodded.

'But when you actually start thinking about it— there's something rather cock-eyed in his reasoning when a man wants out of a marriage to the woman he loves, merely in order to marry her all over again— if she'll have him—and this time for all the right reasons. Wouldn't you agree?'

She was looking at him, but his face had become slightly blurred, and there was also an uncomfortable—almost painful—sensation in the region of her lungs to contend with.

'I...' The word came out as a small croak, so she tried again. This time no sound whatever emerged.

'OK,' he sighed. 'If the idea of marriage to me doesn't appeal, we'll get a divorce and just live——'

'No!' she exclaimed, her powers of speech miraculously restored as she flung herself against him. 'I want to be married to you more than anything!'

'But you *are* married to me,' he said softly with a chuckle.

'Yes, but you always said you wanted it annulled,' she protested, pressing her face tightly against him and praying the tears inexplicably flooding her cheeks would go away as unobtrusively as they had arrived. 'Even when you spoke about us working things out . . . it was conditional on the marriage first being ended.'

'I know. It seems I said rather a lot of stupid things,' he murmured complacently, his lips nuzzling in soft exploration against the wetness of her cheeks. 'Would you mind switching off the waterworks, Carlisle? I'm about to propose.'

'Just ignore them—that's what I'm doing. They're merely a by-product of a surfeit of overwhelming happiness,' she explained contentedly. 'And anyway, how can you propose? We're already married.'

'I was planning on wording that would take that minor obstacle into account,' he said with a chuckle. 'Don't you think I should remove my sweater, before it starts shrinking from this deluge of happiness to which it's being subjected?'

'Only after I've heard this suitably worded proposal.'

'Perhaps there are no suitable words,' he told her softly, drawing back her head till he was gazing down at her, his eyes alive with love. 'Except that I want you for my wife, now and for always . . . that in my heart you've been nothing less for so very long now.'

She was trying to say something, but all that escaped her was a sharp gasp of longing as his hands began moving sensuously against her body.

'Do you know of a decent jeweller?' he asked, his attempts at rendering his voice deadpan not wholly succeeding. 'We'll need a ring or two.'

'A ring or two?' she echoed in choked breathlessness, the sudden surge of happiness in her using up what little breath left in her thanks to the havoc-wreaking excitement being created by his hands.

'You know, wedding-rings and the like. Tell me, Mrs Carlisle, how would you feel about our rounding up family and friends and having a little ceremony—a proper renewing of our marriage vows?' Seemingly oblivious of the major struggle she was having to find words to express her giddy feelings of joy at such a suggestion, he continued, 'Our respective clans would have a chance to meet, and it should go some way to appeasing José and Fred—I'm not quite convinced they really believe you exist. So, what do you think?'

'What do I think?' she croaked, through laughter and tears. 'I think ... I think you have the most stunningly wonderful, romantic ideas!'

'I do rather, don't I?' he agreed modestly, lowering his head to hers, his teeth biting softly on her earlobe. 'Hey, Carlisle, what *are* you doing?' he protested as his nibbling was interrupted by his sweater being yanked over his head.

'Just removing this soggy garment of yours,' she explained cheerfully.

'And I shan't object if there are further liberties you feel like taking,' he whispered huskily, his hands giving her a few pointers as to what sort of liberties he had in mind by deftly removing her blouse and bringing small, shivered gasps of pleasure bursting from her. 'In fact, I'm looking forward to your taking all the liberties you wish with me . . . for the rest of our lives.'

'For the rest of our lives,' she echoed tremulously. 'You know, for a man who's been known to call a spade a shovel, you have the most beautiful way with words, my darling husband.'

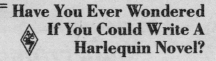

Have You Ever Wondered If You Could Write A Harlequin Novel?

Here's great news—Harlequin is offering a series of cassette tapes to help you do just that. Written by Harlequin editors, these tapes give practical advice on how to make your characters—and your story—come alive. There's a tape for each contemporary romance series Harlequin publishes.

Mail order only

All sales final

Clip this coupon and return to:

HARLEQUIN READER SERVICE
Audiocassette Tape Offer
3010 Walden Ave.
P.O. Box 1396
Buffalo, NY 14269-1396

I enclose my check/money order payable to HARLEQUIN READER SERVICE for $5.70 ($4.95 + 75¢ for delivery) for EACH tape ordered. My total check is for $ _____ .
Please send me:

☐ Romance and Presents   ☐ Intrigue
☐ American Romance   ☐ Temptation
☐ Superromance   ☐ All five tapes ($21.95 total)

Name: _____

Address: _____ Apt: _____

City: _____ State: _____ Zip: _____

NY residents add appropriate sales tax.   AUDIO-H1D

Harlequin Superromance®

Available in Superromance this month
#462—STARLIT PROMISE

STARLIT PROMISE is a deeply moving story of a
woman coming to terms with her grief and gradually
opening her heart to life and love.

Author Petra Holland sets the scene beautifully, never
allowing her heroine to become mired in self-pity. It
is a story that will touch your heart and leave you
celebrating the strength of the human spirit.

Available wherever Harlequin books
are sold.